HEART OF GOLD

LACY WILLIAMS

CHAPTER 1

Tom Seymour had never seen the inside of a jail cell before.

He'd had close calls with the law many times, but Lady Luck had always been on his side.

She'd kept him alive before. He was waiting for her to show up.

Anytime now.

The cell was small and cramped for certain, but it was clean and didn't smell of unwashed bodies. The cot wasn't lined with fleas. He'd even had a decent breakfast—though it had been on the cold side. He was out of the elements, not sleeping under the slate-gray sky in the cold wind.

But it didn't matter that his stay hadn't been unpleasant.

Tom had no intention of spending the rest of his life in a cell.

A page rustled from outside the steel bars.

Tom didn't glance that direction. The dark-haired deputy sitting at the desk across the room had ignored Tom for most of the morning, engrossed in a newspaper. Twice, when Tom had tried to engage him in conversation, the deputy had given one-word answers, not even looking up from his reading.

Tom wasn't discouraged. He'd keep working the problem—being stuck in this ten-by-six cell—until he found a way out. He just had to be patient.

He'd planned his escape for almost a year. He'd gotten free of his two older brothers, although he'd almost died in the process. He could get free of one little jail cell.

And then he was going to find the gold hidden up in the Medicine Bow foothills and disappear. Start over somewhere where nobody knew him.

The outer door opened, and a cold wind blustered inside before it closed again. A familiar figure strode into the combination sheriff's office and jail. Walt White.

The U.S. Marshal who'd found himself in the middle of Tom's attempt at escaping from his brothers.

Tom sat up.

Or he meant to, but the wound in his side protested, and he was both sweating and clammy by the time he'd pushed upright until he leaned against the wall in a sitting position.

As long as he didn't move, he could almost forget that he'd nearly died two days before, riding a runaway horse off the side of a cliff. He could've died during the fall into frigid river water, but he'd walked away with only a fractured wrist and a coupla broken ribs.

Plus the still-healing gunshot wound.

The marshal ignored Tom and walked to the deputy's desk. "He try anything?"

Tom guessed he should feel some indignation, but he was simply too spent to muster it.

The deputy put down his newspaper and gave White his attention. "Aside from two lousy jokes, not a thing. You think he could get far in his condition?"

White's brown-eyed gaze flicked to Tom but didn't linger. "You'd be surprised."

But White wouldn't. Tom heard his unspoken words.

A hint of pride puffed out Tom's chest. Sure enough, if he could get free of these bars, no one would find him. Not even the high falutin' marshal would be able to catch up.

He'd already be gone if not for his injuries.

The broken wrist was an annoyance. He couldn't shave himself, couldn't wash properly, and could barely dress himself. The cast was bulky and got in the way constantly.

But it was a tiny bullet that had nearly cost his life. When the infection from his wound had spread, a high fever had overtaken him.

Lady Luck had kept him alive.

And if she was on his side, he planned to court her favor as long as he could.

He just needed one chance.

It came when the outer door opened again and White's younger sister swept inside.

Ida White hadn't looked like *this* the last time Tom had seen her. She'd been bedraggled after she'd fished him out of that river, her dress wrinkled and muddy as she'd worked to keep them alive in the elements. It'd been almost twenty-four hours before they'd been found by a search party-slash-posse.

Now, she looked like a vision in a dark blue calico with little white flowers. She untangled a scarf around her neck and hung it and the wool overcoat she wore on a hook near the door. Her hair was up in a twist behind her head. She looked fresh and hale, but she wasn't smiling.

That was fine.

She was here, and he could work with that.

White crossed to his sister and murmured something Tom couldn't make out. Her lips firmed in a line, and she nodded tightly.

And then the two of them crossed to Tom's cell.

Walt unlocked the door and opened it, leaving it that way. "You try anything, and you'll have a second gunshot wound to match the first."

Tom swallowed the retort that formed in his mouth. *Tread carefully.* He held White's stare until the other man shook his head and turned away.

Ida ignored both of them and stepped through the door and over to Tom. "How's your pain?"

"I wouldn't feel a thing if you'd give me a smile." He said the words at a volume her brother wouldn't be able to hear, even though the marshal was lingering close to the cell door.

Ida shot him a sharp look but didn't respond as she reached inside a satchel she carried. "Your wrist?"

He shook his head. The ache was a dull roar. Different than the piercing pain in his side, which had faded some since the worst of the infection had passed.

"And your side?"

He shook his head again. He wouldn't give the marshal the satisfaction of knowing Tom was in near-constant agony.

"You look like you haven't slept," she murmured.

"You look captivating."

That sharp look returned.

At this proximity, he could see the tiny lines fanning her eyes. As if maybe she hadn't slept well either.

And the fading bruise on the underside of her jaw. Hector had given her that, striking her in anger during the hours he'd held her captive.

Tom was sorry for that.

"Can you unbutton your shirt so I can attend your wound?"

He raised his casted hand, hiding a wince when the movement pulled something in his side. "Afraid not."

Her lips pinched. But she didn't call him on his bluff.

Admittedly, he could've unbuttoned his shirt. It just would've taken ten times as long as it should.

He hated looking unkempt. Hated that his hair wasn't combed. Hated that he didn't have one of his fine suits to wear. When he'd changed out of his icy, still-wet clothes, he'd been offered hand-me-down clothes that were a size too large—brown pair of pants and a shirt that had once been white. It was this or nothing.

She didn't seem to notice as she perched on the edge of his cot and efficiently undid the buttons of his shirt. She left the top two buttoned and swept aside the rest of the material.

This close, he got a whiff of flour and cinnamon and imagined her in the kitchen earlier that morning. She would make a picture putting a pie in the oven.

Her attention was on the dressing covering his wound, and he let himself study her. She had fine wisps of hair escaping their confinement and curling around her ear. Her lashes were long and fluttered as she concentrated on removing his bandage.

Even the smallest brush of her fingers sent pain radiating through his side and he needed to distract himself as she re-bandaged the wound, apparently satisfied with how it looked.

"Do you usually make house calls to the jail?" he asked.

She ignored him.

"I guess a town this small doesn't see too much excitement." There were only two cells in the joint.

She rifled in her bag, her face averted.

"You don't wanna talk to me? I thought we were friends."

Her gaze climbed to his face, but her eyes were shuttered and revealed nothing. "It's the twenty-third of December. I'd much rather be home with my family, making Christmas candies. The only reason I'm here today is as a favor to my older brother—the town doctor."

She didn't button his shirt again, and he saw her hands shaking as she stuffed the unused bandages back into her satchel.

This was the last thing he needed—distance between them. Her uncertainty. Or was it fear?

He stopped her retreat with a touch on her wrist.

"My brothers didn't think we were playactin'," he said quietly. "And they're still out there. They'll come for me, and they'll figure out that you're nearby. When they spring me, they'll probably come for you, too."

It was a lie. All of it. His brothers had seen him go off that cliff, he was sure of it. With the law closing in, Hector and Tristan would have left the area, believing him dead.

But if she could convince her tin star brother to move him, Tom would have a shot at escaping.

He put on a grave, concerned expression. "I'm

not trying to scare you. You'll want to be safe when they get here."

———————

IDA'S HANDS shook as she slipped into her coat and wound her scarf around her neck. She purposely kept her gaze from straying to the cell where Tom Seymour was propped against the wall where she'd left him.

The man drove her crazy. He made a show of being relaxed, staring at her with heavy-lidded eyes and that enigmatic smile.

But she'd been close enough to see the way the skin near his lips had whitened when she'd probed the flesh around his wound.

He hadn't said a word.

The words he *had said*...

"Can I talk to you for a moment outside?" she asked her brother. She hadn't meant to interrupt his chat with deputy Miles Fletcher, but she couldn't stay in this room a moment longer.

It was snowing. A cold wind blew straight through her coat as she stepped through the door, Walt behind her. She crossed her arms over her middle.

Walt's concerned gaze skimmed her face. "Are you all right? What did he say to you?"

He said we were friends.

She swallowed against her tumultuous emotions and tried to keep her voice from shaking.

"He said that his brothers would come for him again. That they saw us together plenty and they might come for me too."

After she'd witnessed the Seymour brothers take Walt and Ida's best friend Libby hostage off a home-bound train, she'd gone after them. Managed to get herself captured too, and spent three days tied up, starved, and terrified by Tristan and Hector Seymour, Tom's older brothers. When she'd been separated from Walt and Libby, Tom had convinced her that if she wanted to stay alive, she should pretend to be sweet on him.

She'd faked feelings for Tom only out of self-preservation.

And now her actions were coming back to haunt her.

Her hands tightened into fists. She couldn't help the reaction, thinking about everything that had happened. Maybe Walt wouldn't see, since her hands were hidden beneath her elbows.

It didn't matter anyway, because he pulled her

into a hug, tucking her against his chest and rubbing her back.

She inhaled a shaky breath. One good thing had come of this ordeal. She'd gotten her brother back.

"The Seymours think Tom's dead," Walt reminded her. "Matty and I saw their tracks heading up into the mountains. They were goin' after that lost gold."

She knew that. Walt had reassured both her and her best friend Libby—his sweetheart now—that the Seymours were long gone. Ida and her friend were safe.

But just because the two outlaws had run into the mountains didn't mean they'd stay there.

Ida could still feel the pure terror she'd experienced when Hector Seymour had struck her across the face for standing up to him. She'd been sure the man would kill her when his friend had died— another outlaw, who'd been burned in the train explosion they'd caused.

Ida had never been hit before, not even accidently when she'd rough-housed with her brothers as a child.

She'd pretended to be this brave, fierce woman. But she wasn't. Not at all.

Only Tom's quick thinking had kept her alive.

But she wasn't kidding herself. He'd had some

ulterior motive for doing so. Something he wouldn't tell her. Or Walt. Or anyone.

Tom wasn't her friend. His only interest was in saving his own hide.

Walt eased back, his arms dropping. "I'm sorry I made you come into town for this."

"It's fine." But she had to blink rapidly to keep tears from falling. It was annoying, really. She hadn't cried once during the days she'd been held against her will by the outlaw gang. But now that it was over, she'd turned into a regular watering pot.

She knew Walt would've preferred their older brother Maxwell tend to Tom. But Hattie, Maxwell's wife, had fallen ill recently, and Maxwell was overworked already trying to care for her and see patients at the clinic.

Libby had offered to come with her, but Walt's sweetheart had been just as traumatized as Ida had over the past week, so Ida had insisted she stay on the family ranch.

Libby couldn't see through her like Walt could. Even though her brother had been away from home for years, they'd easily fallen back into the close relationship they'd shared growing up.

But Walt didn't know everything. He didn't know about the kiss she and Tom had shared, back in the outlaw hideout. No one did.

And she meant to keep it that way.

"No one's coming after you," Walt reassured her with a hand at her elbow. "I wouldn't let them get within a hundred yards of you. Neither would Pa, or Matty, or Oscar."

"Or Edgar or Davy. I know." She was even able to smile about it.

At home, she was surrounded by protective older brothers and their families. But what about when she left? She'd had grand plans to take a job as a traveling nurse.

Right now, she couldn't stomach the thought of boarding a train again.

"Everything will be fine," Walt said. "Do you need me to take you home?"

"No. I told Velma I'd meet her at the general store." She'd ridden to town in the wagon with her twenty-one-year-old niece.

Walt kissed her cheek. "Then I'll see you at home tonight."

"Be safe."

He stepped back inside the jailhouse and she began walking toward the general store.

Everything will be fine. Maybe it was because he'd been a lawman for years that the words rolled so easily from his tongue.

Ida was the one who shivered beneath her quilt

at night, unable to fall asleep.

Even Bear Creek wasn't the same since the incident. She'd walked this boardwalk weekly for her entire life.

She waved at Martha Vandenheimer, sweeping in front of the milliner's. She'd known the woman for as long as she could remember.

But following Walt off that train, being taken hostage by the Seymours... Something had broken inside her.

She couldn't stop her eyes from darting to every shadow between building fronts. Her chest was tight, her heart beating faster than normal.

She was a mess.

And she felt all alone.

No one could see her turmoil. Each person she passed, from the young man outside the butcher's to the blacksmith working the forge, was busy with tasks and unaware that danger could be lurking just around the corner.

There was a wreath wrapped in red ribbon hanging on a post in front of the general store.

The reminder that Christmas was only two days away made Ida feel... nothing.

She was broken, and she didn't know how to stitch herself back together.

Would she ever be whole again?

CHAPTER 2

Ida woke to the sensation of falling, falling into icy water that closed over her head.

She blinked a few times and recognized the shadowy shapes of her own bedroom. She was gasping and trembling and had huddled so far beneath the quilt that it must've covered her face and contributed to the frightening nightmare. Was it still called a nightmare if it was a memory?

She held her breath for a moment to check that Libby still slept in the bed next to her. Her friend breathed evenly and slowly. Good. Ida had only terrified herself.

The windowpane rattled, and she jumped. But it was only the wind howling.

Ida's body ached. She hadn't been asleep for long. She stood, pulled on a wrapper over her long nightgown, and untucked her braid before she padded to the door. When she opened it, she found there was lamplight shining from the kitchen down the hall. Someone was still awake.

She glanced over her shoulder into the darkened room. She couldn't bear facing her bed again, not yet, so she slipped out. There were certain family members who she wouldn't care to see right then, but if it was only her mother, Ida would warm some milk and try to breathe until the nightmare receded.

It wasn't Mama, but as Ida tiptoed across the living room, she heard the familiar cadence of Papa's voice, and tears pricked behind her eyes. She could use a hug.

She passed by the long dining table that had been stationed in the living room for as long as she could remember. With such a big family, the kitchen was only used for preparing the meals, not eating them.

She heard the murmur of a second voice and stopped in the shadows outside the kitchen doorway. From this angle, she could see both Walt and Matty leaning against the counter. Pa stood nearby, his back to her. There were coffee cups pushed aside, as if the trio had been chatting for a while. Long enough for the coffee to be drunk or get cold.

"I can't ask it of Ida," Walt said. He looked so serious that her stomach twisted.

Ask what from her?

"She's stronger than you think," Pa said. It wasn't only the confidence of his quiet words that warmed her. Pa was never rattled. As long as she'd stayed under his roof, she'd been safe.

But Walt's next words made that protected feeling dissipate like the illusion it was.

"You can't know what it was like for her out there." Walt shook his head. "They were threatening her life while she tried to save one of them. They are monsters. She's shaken up, even if she won't admit to it."

The Seymours. They were talking about what had happened.

She'd thought they'd talked it to death over the past days. She'd had to give an accounting of every moment since the outlaws had stepped onto that train and Walt and Libby had been taken hostage.

Walt ran both hands over his face. She'd known he felt guilty about what happened, even though he couldn't have prevented any of it. He still carried it now.

"If you're determined to go with Libby to visit her parents, it's the only choice that makes sense." This from Matty, who'd been a deputy in Bear

Creek since Ida had been a child. Her brother said the words almost in an exasperated way, as if they'd been over this already. "He's the only man in custody, and he's not like one of our usuals. He doesn't need to sleep off a night of too much drink. My deputies want to spend their Christmases at home with their families, just like you want to spend it with Libby. If we bring Seymour here, I can keep a close eye on him. With all of us together, he'll never have a moment alone."

"No chance to escape," Pa added.

Seymour. Tom. They were talking about bringing Tom here, to the family homestead.

Walt had made no secret of his plans to get Tom on a train to face justice in front of a judge in Colorado. But meeting Libby and the ordeal the three of them had gone through had changed her brother. Gone was his single-mindedness, his urgency to get the outlaw behind prison bars. He still wanted that. But Libby needed him. She was traveling home to see her parents for the first time in years. It would be an emotional reunion and Walt wanted to be with her.

Ida understood Walt's dilemma. There was also the fact that Tristan and Hector Seymour were still at large and had tried to rescue their brother from Walt's custody once. One deputy watching over

Tom in an unprotected jailhouse in town wasn't enough. The Seymour brothers wouldn't care whether it was Christmas or not. They'd kill anyone in their way.

She'd seen enough death over the past week.

If Walt and Matty thought it was safer for everyone involved to move Tom to the homestead for a couple of days, she wasn't going to stand in their way.

She cleared her throat and then stepped into the kitchen. All three pairs of eyes flicked to her.

"I woke up and thought maybe some warm milk would help me get back to sleep." She crossed to the cool box and bent to retrieve the milk. "I couldn't help overhearing." It was easier to say when she turned her back to the men and faced the stove and the shallow pan there. "I agree with Matty. Of course it makes sense to hold Tom... Seymour"—she stumbled over his name—"here for a few days."

"Ida—"

Walt was the one who started to object, but she caught Pa's hand gesture from the corner of her eye and her brother went silent.

"You won't even have to see him," her father said.

"Don't be silly." She chided him gently. The house would be full of distractions over the next few days. Cecilia and her husband and their girls were due to arrive tomorrow. Ricky and his family were coming down from up north near Sheridan. Mama already had lists upon lists of things to do in the kitchen. Meals to prepare and items to bake and gifts for their neighbors and friends. There would be presents exchanged and games played and not a moment's rest.

But even with the house completely full, there wouldn't be enough room for her to avoid Tom completely.

She wouldn't let it matter. "I'll be fine. And you don't need to worry about Tom, Walt. I doubt your prisoner is up to any kind of escape attempt. He could barely move when I saw him earlier."

The milk was bubbling in the pan and she scooted it off the burner. No need to scorch it and show them just how rattled she was. Pa handed her a mug, and she accepted it gratefully.

Her father held her gaze. She wondered how much he saw. Probably too much. "You don't need to worry about anything," he said in his quiet, steady way. "Just enjoy Christmas with the family."

She smiled and hid her trembling lips behind her mug as she took a sip.

She excused herself and went back down the hall to stand silently inside the door of the room she shared with Libby.

The darkened room made her shiver, and she gulped the milk.

Enjoy.

There would be no enjoyment in this holiday. She could only pray it passed quickly.

———

LADY LUCK WAS INDEED SMILING on Tom.

He'd woken this morning even more stiff and sore than before. How could that be possible?

But while he'd been eating cold scrambled eggs —left-handed and badly—the marshal had entered the jailhouse with another deputy, a man a decade his senior. Tom vaguely recognized the man but couldn't name him.

Turned out the deputy was Walt's older brother, Matty. Who looked nothing like Walt. No resemblance whatsoever.

The Marshal had only stayed long enough to deliver news and a warning.

It was a Christmas Eve miracle. Tom was being moved to the White family's large ranch. He'd stay over the holiday, and once the marshal returned home—from where, Tom didn't know—Tom would be delivered to a judge who'd no doubt sentence him to prison he had no intention of visiting.

The way he figured it, he had forty-eight hours to get loose of the White family and get outta Dodge.

He must've scared Ida well and good with his reminder that his brothers were still out there. Whatever the reason Walt had come to his decision, Tom was thankful.

His excitement waned when deputy Matty trussed him up in leg irons. Tom pretended indifference but doubted the man was fooled. He figured the only reason he didn't have a matching set of handcuffs was the cast on his wrist.

And then Matty laid him out in a wagon bed like an invalid. He was warm enough with a hot brick from the stove and a coupla blankets, but that wasn't how he wanted to arrive.

He'd rather have dressed himself in a sharp suit and shaved. It would've made a much better impression.

As it was, he couldn't even sit up. The doc— another of Ida's brothers, this one dark-haired and green eyed—had checked him out that morning and pronounced him well enough to travel. But the muscles all up and down Tom's side still protested movement.

Shouldn't he be feeling better by now? Have more mobility?

That didn't matter. Even if he had to limp or crawl, he was getting out of there. Except the dark-haired deputy from the jailhouse rode alongside the wagon on horseback. Mighty hard for Tom to crawl away without being noticed with a second deputy along.

He did his best to keep track of how long they'd traveled. Maybe ninety minutes out of town?

The wagon wheels crossed a particularly large rut, and he was jostled so badly that he had to bite back a cry. He tried to breathe through it, eyes going to the unbroken blue sky.

And then the wagon rolled to a stop.

He used his one good hand to push himself to a sitting position. He might be weak as a newborn kitten, but he didn't want anyone to know it.

"This him?" The voice belonged to a boy who might be all of seventeen. The teen could've been the marshal's doppelgänger if he were a few years older. As it was, he sat tall in the saddle of a paint pony, so slender beneath his slicker and hat that it seemed like a strong gust of wind would blow him away.

"He don't look so good." The boy dismounted and stepped forward, reaching for the tailgate latch.

Tom didn't take offense as he threw off the blanket and made to scoot to the end of the wagon.

If he looked half as haggard as he felt, he must be a sight indeed.

He threw the boy as charming a smile as he could muster. "Tom Seymour."

He received a scathing look. "Stay away from my sisters and my ma."

"This is Andrew," Matty said. He almost sounded...gleeful. The deputy hopped from the wagon seat and rounded the conveyance to come to Tom's other side. It took both of them holding him by his upper arms to ease him down until his boots touched the ground. He couldn't help the hiss of air that escaped between his teeth as he straightened. If the two men heard it, they didn't comment.

"Everyone out here will be watching you closer than an ant beneath a magnifying glass," Andrew muttered.

The kid was angry.

Tom wasn't surprised. He'd never come face-to-face with anyone after he and his brothers had taken what they wanted. He'd only seen the faces of dismay, shock and anger from a distance as they'd made their getaway.

He wouldn't get any help from Andrew, but maybe he could be useful. Time would tell.

They shifted him, and he got his first look at the ranch house.

He didn't know what he'd expected, but it wasn't the mishmash of a building that had obviously once been a smaller cabin. He'd guessed the wings had been added at different times. There was another building across the yard and a barn not far beyond that. Another house, this one smaller, was tucked on a hillside a quarter mile beyond the ranch house.

A tall tree stood sentinel behind the main residence. It even had a swing hanging from one high branch. How idyllic.

His heart leapt to see Ida on the porch. Had she come out to greet him? No. The dark-haired deputy stood on the first step, his head a foot lower than hers.

She was smiling at the deputy, a welcoming smile that made Tom's gut twist in a way he'd never felt before.

Matty nudged him forward, and he took a step— or tried to. He'd forgotten for a moment about the leg irons, and what would've been his natural stride was tethered. He teetered for a moment before he caught his balance. He moved at an awkward shuffling gait that felt like a snail's crawl.

By the time they reached the porch, he was flushed and sweating after the exertion of walking only a few yards.

How was he supposed to navigate the steps with shackles on?

"...some of the younger folks in town are getting together for a social early in the new year." This from the young deputy who'd barely given Tom the time of day in that jail cell. Tom was surprised the man could string together that many words.

Ida wasn't surprised. She was still smiling at him. "That sounds like fun."

"I'll take you, if you want to go," Andrew added.

"We'll see. I may take a job"—she slanted a look at Tom—"somewhere out of town."

"Be a shame if you leave," Tom said. "Hello, friend." He winked at her as if he'd had a bath and a shave and they were meeting over a cup of cider at the social she wanted to attend.

Her smile slipped. It was slight, so slight that her brothers didn't seem to notice. A half-step behind Tom, Matty murmured something about their mama.

Ida spoke to Tom. "You're gray around the edges. That wagon was real comfortable, huh? You'd better come in and sit by the fire. I'll grab you a cup of coffee."

That was enough incentive for him to attempt the first step in the restrictive leg irons. It was touch-and-go, but he made it up the four steps and onto the porch.

"He's not a guest," Andrew remarked in a tight voice. "You don't have to wait on him."

Ida glanced over her shoulder just before she passed through the doorway. "Of course he isn't. But he's injured and I have a duty to see that he's healing."

Her words were breezy as Tom rattled along behind her in his chains.

Andrew and Matty followed him while the deputy called out a goodbye.

She led him to a wingback chair closest to the fire and he sat, pretending as his ribs pulled that he wasn't biting back another cry.

She saw it. Her eyes glittered before she turned and bustled into the kitchen.

The two men spoke in low voices across the room. It was a big space, large enough for the sofa and a couple of chairs, plus the long dining table with hewn wooden benches along the wall nearest the kitchen.

There was more movement from somewhere else in the house. The murmur of a female voice.

Ida was back in a moment, carrying a steaming mug. She handed it to him as if he were a neighbor stopping by for a visit.

She was pretending.

She didn't like him being here. He didn't think she was afraid of him—he'd seen her toughness and fire out in the wilderness. But she was wary and uncomfortable.

She didn't fool him with her smiles.

He could see right through her.

CHAPTER 3

The leg irons stayed on.

But Tom wasn't locked in a bedroom like he expected. He remained in that chair in the living room.

He hadn't seen a handoff for the keys, but surely the deputy brother had given them to someone in the house. Was he expected to keep them on at all hours? Sleep with them on?

The last thing he wanted was for his irritation to show. Matty had disappeared. Young Andrew stood at attention across the room, watching Tom drink his coffee.

At least the room was warm.

Ida bustled around in the kitchen. Every once in awhile he saw her pass by the doorway. He heard the door open beyond her and the murmur of a man's voice. Then the rustle of clothing—maybe a coat?—and the sound of someone washing up.

He stood up without jarring his side too badly.

Andrew bristled immediately. It was almost comical how much he resembled Walt, even in mannerisms.

An older man came through the doorway, quickly surveying the room. He crossed to where Tom stood. "I'm Jonas White. Welcome to my home."

He held out his right hand for Tom to shake. Though his words were friendly, there was something hard about his eyes.

Tom couldn't shake his hand, not with the cast on. Ida's father recognized it, too, because he wasn't surprised when Tom reached out with his left hand for an awkward handshake.

"He stood up like he was goin' somewhere," Andrew muttered from across the room.

"To the kitchen." Tom picked up the empty tin the coffee'd been in.

Jonas scrutinized him. "I told my daughter she didn't have to see you if she didn't want to. I'll take that and you can stretch your legs in here."

"Papa." Ida appeared in the doorway. She had something gathered up in her apron and moved to the table. "I told you, I'm fine. He can come in the kitchen if he wants."

See? She was fine.

At the table, she lowered her apron and a pile of walnuts spilled onto the table. One rolled across and onto the floor before she could stop it.

But Jonas's stare remained on Tom, assessing him. It wasn't comfortable. Ida's father knew who Tom was, knew his reputation. Tom wasn't spinning a story like when he'd originally met Walt years before, pretending to be a ranch hand.

Ida crossed to her younger brother. "If you're going to hover, you can be useful by shelling these." She held out a small silver tool.

Andrew scowled but snatched it from her.

Tom followed Ida into the kitchen, cursing the shackles that hobbled his every step. Andrew was left behind, the repetitive *snick* of his task fading as Tom moved into the kitchen.

Jonas was on his heels, probably impatient at how slowly Tom moved.

Ida stood next to a wide cookstove. She was using a kitchen towel to protect her hand as she lifted the lid off of a large pot. She stirred whatever was inside and then replaced the lid.

"I suppose you'd better put us to work." Jonas

moved easily to the counter and left the tin near some other dishes.

Ida's gaze slipped briefly over Tom, not settling.

"What are you making next?" Jonas asked.

"I thought we'd better start popping some corn." She tipped her head in Tom's direction. "I doubt he can help much, but watching corn... That he might be able to handle."

Hey. He felt the urge to protest the fact that they were talking about him as if he weren't present. But he kept quiet.

She moved a skillet onto the stove, and he watched from the middle of the room as she poured oil in it. She laid out a cup and a long wooden spoon within arms' reach, then moved past Tom to grab a silver pail of dried out corn kernels, which she set on the counter.

It was not a small pail.

"How much corn are you planning to pop?" Tom asked.

"Buckets." Andrews voice carried from the other room. Either he didn't want to be left out, or he wanted Tom to know he was still paying attention.

"Who is going to eat all of this?" Tom asked.

Ida and her father shared a smile.

"We're not eating it," she said. She still wasn't

looking at him. "We'll make garlands to hang on the tree."

What tree? But he didn't ask. "How many garlands?"

"Enough for the children to hang."

Ida motioned him closer, and he couldn't help but notice how her gaze fell to his feet when it took him twice as long to shuffle over. "You've made popcorn before?"

He shook his head. "'Fraid not."

Something flickered in her expression, but she averted her gaze so quickly that he couldn't read it.

His eyes lingered on the curve of her cheek. She was beautiful. What would've happened if they'd met a month later? In a different place? Under different circumstances?

Ida used the cup to measure out some kernels and toss them into the skillet, quickly covering it with a lid. She used the handle to shake the pan horizontally before she let it sit back on the stove. Then she pushed the cloth into his good hand, avoiding eye contact with him. "You'll want to shake the pan every so often so the kernels don't stick. You'll hear it when the corn starts to pop. Once it stops, I'll come switch out the popped kernels, and we'll start all over."

He couldn't help but be amused. "So... you want me to stand here and hold this pan?"

Now he received a little flash of fire in her eyes, but her voice was even when she spoke. "I want you to shake it at intervals. Unless you'd rather go lie in bed like an invalid, yes."

She whirled away before he could respond.

"Mama also had vanilla candy on her list," she said to her father. "Do you want to start separating out egg whites?"

Something pinged against the inside of the pan, and Tom startled, turning toward Ida to make sure nothing was wrong. *Ping. Ping.* More kernels went off, and he caught the twitch of her lips before she turned away. Had she seen him jump at the unexpected sound?

Jonas pulled two bowls and a whisk from beneath another long counter.

Ida set a bowl of eggs beside him.

"Shake the pan," Ida ordered.

Tom had already forgotten his orders. He flipped the towel over his hand as best he could and gave the pan a good shake. He hid a wince at the motion.

The kernels were creating quite a racket now.

He was shocked when he glanced back at Jonas and saw the man easily cracking an egg and using the two halves of the shell to separate the whites into a large bowl.

"You know your way around the kitchen," he said.

A woman with smile lines around her eyes and streaks of gray in her auburn hair—Ida's mother?—entered the room. She must've heard Tom's comment, because she smiled. "I'm afraid the children would've starved to death in the beginning if it weren't for Jonas and his cooking skills."

She crossed to her husband and bussed a kiss on his cheek. She murmured something in his ear and he responded, though Tom couldn't hear anything over the racket of the corn popping.

When he glanced at Ida, he caught her watching him.

He should've winked. Or said something charming to make her laugh.

But an uncomfortable feeling in his chest made him look away.

———

IDA WATCHED Tom sneak furtive glances at her parents. His expression showed a mix of curiosity and... disgruntlement.

Good.

Now she wasn't the only uncomfortable one.

She pulled out several oranges and brought them to the table. At her movement, Tom's glance slipped to her, his expression smoothing out.

What was it about her parents that bothered him?

She was used to their easy affection. She'd grown up in a home where it was customary for her father and mother to sit close together on the sofa after a long day of work. They shared cups of coffee and warm conversation. She'd seen Mama comfort Papa over the loss of one of the stock animals. Papa had spent hours upon hours in the wagon when Ida's maternal grandmother had been sick and Mama had needed to travel to spend time with her.

She'd never once questioned her parents' love for each other.

Tom's half-embarrassed expression made her wonder. What were his parents like? What possessed a man to follow his brothers into a life of crime?

Tom was distracted by Mama and Papa and hadn't noticed that the popcorn had slowed its popping. It wouldn't take long to scorch.

She quickly moved to the stove. He stepped aside as she removed the pan lid and poured out the popcorn into a waiting bowl.

"Are your parents still alive?" She kept her eyes on what she was doing as she asked it.

From the corner of her eye, she saw him shake his head. She also saw him steal another glance at Mama and Papa, now discussing whether they needed more eggs for the candy. He almost looked... pained.

She refilled the pan with corn and slapped the lid on quickly because, now that it was hot, the next batch would pop more quickly.

"I don't remember them," Tom said quietly. "It was always just my brothers."

There was a strange note to his voice, one she hadn't heard before. Was she supposed to take pity on him? Or was he playing on her sympathy?

Even as her suspicion ran rampant, a part of her shuddered to imagine a small boy growing up with older brothers like Hector and Tristan Seymour.

Would they have had any shred of compassion if Tom were tired or hungry? She'd only seen violence and evil from the two men. Tristan hadn't shown mercy when he'd punched a man in the train car for disobeying his orders. He'd hit Ida when she'd dared stand up to him. He'd threatened to kill her more than once.

She hated to think of a little boy enduring the same. It hurt to imagine it. Her brothers could be overprotective and annoying at times, like Andrew hovering in the next room just now. But she'd always known that they loved her.

Tom shook the pan and she blinked out of her thoughts. She hadn't even noticed how loud the popping had become.

"What's in that one?" He hitched his chin to indicate the large pot at the back of the stove.

"Apple cider," she said. "Or it will be in a few hours." Even now, the scent of warm apples and cinnamon and cloves filled the room.

"And the walnuts?"

"They'll be used in candy. A gift for our neighbors and friends."

He was silent for a moment. Then, "I've never done anything like this before. "

What would it be like to grow up in a different family? To have a different life? Would she have been a different person? Undoubtedly so. But did that mean that Tom didn't deserve to be blamed for the crimes he'd committed?

Her head hurt and she raised a hand to rub her forehead, turning away from him. The orange candy wasn't going to make itself.

Mama had set to work peeling potatoes for supper. Just because her hands were busy, it didn't stop her from glancing at Tom. "Ida said your injuries were significant. I've got your room made up, so just say something if you need to lie down."

Tom looked genuinely surprised. "I'm staying in the house? Not out in the bunkhouse? Or the barn?"

"We can keep an eye on you better from here," Andrew called out.

Tom didn't bat an eye or show any reaction. He was watching everything.

The popcorn was ready to change again, and Ida moved to the stove. This time, Tom took only half a step back, which meant that she was far too close to him as she reached for the pan.

"It's almost like Andrew's forgotten I saved your life." His murmur was for her ears only.

She hadn't forgotten. Not any of it.

"You could've let me go at any time," she whispered as a flush rose in her face. Maybe if he had, she wouldn't be terrified of leaving home again.

Papa and Mama were having their own conversation, not paying attention to them.

"If I let you walk away, Hector would've shot me in the back for it."

She didn't glance at him. She knew what she would see if she did. His voice was earnest, and his expression would match. He wanted her to believe that he'd done the best he could to protect her. Those three days that she'd been trapped by the outlaws had blurred together in a mishmash of terror and cold and darkness.

She handed him back the dish cloth and backed away.

Tom *had* saved her life, even though they'd almost both drowned in that river. He'd thrown her off the horse, while he'd been trapped in the saddle. The event had resulted in his broken ribs and fractured wrist. She could've broken her neck in the fall, but he'd prevented that by getting her clear of the horse.

But that didn't mean they were friends. He'd been with the outlaws, after all.

Hoofbeats sounded outside, accompanied by the jingle of a harness. She was the closest to the window and glanced up to see her sister Breanna bundled beneath a blanket, her blonde hair unbound and blowing like a flag.

"Is that Breanna?" It couldn't be, and yet Ida could see clearly with her own eyes that it was. Adam was beside her, and two tow-headed children bundled behind them in the wagon.

No one had breathed a word about Breanna coming for Christmas.

Ida found her throat choked with tears. It was a near thing, but she beat Andrew to the back door to burst out in the cold and receive the first hug.

CHAPTER 4

I f not for Andrew—and the stinkin' shackles—
Tom could've made a clean getaway.

Ida's older sister was a blonde beauty who
exuded spirit from every pore. She and her husband
and their two small children were welcomed with
hugs and kisses and so many voices talking at the
same time that Tom had a hard time keeping up.

Andrew gave his sister a perfunctory hug and
then stood in the corner with arms crossed, staring
at Tom as if daring him to try anything. There was
certainly enough distraction that he might've
slipped away... if not for the leg irons.

Where was that key? He'd let his eyes roam every
nook and shelf visible in the kitchen but didn't see it
anywhere.

Andrew was so focused on Tom that he didn't seem to notice Ida's emotions overflowing. She'd laughed away the first burst of happy tears as she had embraced her sister. But when she thought no one was looking, she unobtrusively swiped beneath her eyes. It seemed the tears kept coming.

Ida's mother shooed Tom away from where he was surely burning the popcorn. He followed the mass of bodies into the living room and took a hardback chair because it was tucked back in the corner. Out of the way. He didn't get there before Breanna noticed his shackles and cut a quick look to her father.

Andrew went back to the table and continued shelling the walnuts, though he seemed incredibly slow at the task, mostly because of how he kept looking up to glare at Tom.

Who didn't let it bother him. He was more interested in watching the interplay between Ida and Breanna, Breanna and Jonas, the children and everyone. Everyone except Breanna's husband, who'd declined help bringing in the luggage and returned outside.

"You should've told us you were coming," Jonas said. "I would've sent one of your brothers to fetch you from town."

Breanna leaned one hand on her father's shoulder and rose on tiptoe to smack a kiss on his cheek. "That would've ruined the surprise. Ooh, you've started the vanilla candy?"

"Where's Carrie?" asked the little girl, who must've been about five years old.

Her brother, younger but not by much, danced around her.

"Carrie and Albert will be here soon." Ida reached out to tickle the little boy, who danced away with a laugh.

Are you all right? He saw Breanna mouth the words to Ida when her father wasn't looking. Neither woman glanced in his direction, but they didn't have to.

Ida's sister must've been worried about her after what she'd gone through. Worried enough to endure a long train ride with small children to check on her.

The love between the two sisters was easy to see. And it made something shift inside Tom in an uncomfortable way, same as when he'd been in the kitchen with her parents.

Breanna's husband came through, a bag under each arm and one clutched in each hand.

Jonas moved to head him off, but the man shook

his head. "Everyone else is behind me. They'll be looking for you." He headed for the hallway, obviously familiar enough with the home to know where he was going.

For a moment, Tom wondered if Lady Luck had arrived.

If the Whites hosted unexpected family members, maybe he would be forced into the bunkhouse after all.

But he didn't have time to think about his potential escape when, on the heels of Breanna's husband, came more voices, more bodies.

He lost track of the family connections as more than one branch of the family seemed to arrive together. And then another soon after that.

A teen boy joined Andrew at the table, and the two of them took turns glaring at Tom.

Another little girl had joined the two children, and all three ran through the room, dodging the adults and trying to tag each other.

It wasn't long before the popcorn was brought out in bowls and placed at intervals on the long table. Needles and thread were brought out as well, and the children were lured to the table by a couple of teen girls.

Tom kept getting sideways glances, and he was

almost tripped over more than once as the room filled.

He was obviously in the way, an outsider. The men in the room seemed just as hostile as Andrew. Nobody greeted him at all.

It was ridiculous to feel disappointment. He knew that. Everyone in this room knew who he was, even the teen girls who were whispering and stealing glances his way.

After the initial flurry of greetings, Tom began to see the connections between the couples. One wife in a dark green holiday dress brought her husband a cup of coffee. He pressed her hand briefly before she went and rejoined Ida's mother in the kitchen.

Another man couldn't seem to keep his eyes off of his wife, who sat across the room teasing Andrew and his companion, distracting them temporarily.

It was beyond clear that every member of the family loved the others.

He didn't know what that felt like. He was attracted to Ida. He'd definitely felt something during their pretend kiss. But what the people in this room shared was clearly something more. They were comfortable with each other. They knew each other inside and out. And they liked each other.

Watching them opened a hole inside of him. Had

his mama ever looked at him with affection, the way Breanna looked at her daughter when the girl tugged on her skirt?

Surely Tom's mother had cared for him. But what he was witnessing was as foreign to him as if they were speaking another language.

He startled when a small head peeked over the arm of his chair. It was the little blonde boy. His sister scooted up behind him.

"You're not helping," the little boy said.

He looked between them, unsure what that was supposed to mean.

The little girl stuck out her hand. She held a needle and thread clasped in her fist, which she shook.

The boy had a handful of popcorn cupped in his palms.

They wanted him to string popcorn?

"I don't know how to do it," he said.

"It's easy," the little girl said.

"I've only got one hand." Tom lifted his cast to show them that he wouldn't be able to grip anything with his right hand.

The little boy smiled, showing a gap-toothed grin. "We can help you."

How could anyone say no to that?

IDA WAS THRILLED to see her sister, who lived in Boston and traveled all over with her husband, a journalist with a family legacy running one of the largest newspapers in the East. But the distraction wasn't enough to make her forget that Tom was sitting across the room.

She was a little surprised he hadn't used the commotion of everyone's arrival to try to escape.

She took Andrew's chopped walnuts into the kitchen, where Mama needed them for the walnut candy.

Mama nodded her thanks. "Why don't you ask your brother and Leo and Ruth to go cut the tree?"

Andrew wasn't thrilled with the request, shooting a glare at Tom before he acquiesced. He murmured something in Oscar's ear before following Leo and Ruth out the door.

When she looked up, she saw Edith and Archie, Breanna's children, both at Tom's knees.

An initial beat of apprehension was quelled when she realized her sister was surreptitiously watching the children. Tom would be a fool to try something with so many people in the room.

Her feet carried her in that direction without conscious thought.

Edith was instructing him in the way only a bossy five-year-old sister could on how to hold a needle.

Archie was pushing a piece of popcorn onto it and then both children squabbled as they helped Tom pull the corn down the thread.

He glanced up at her as she neared, and she was certain she saw a beat of relief in his eyes.

"Aunt Ida, Mr. Tom has never made a popcorn string before." Edith seemed affronted by this fact. Her brother nodded along.

"Please say you've come to rescue me," Tom murmured from the side of his mouth, the words almost inaudible.

"You look like you're having fun." He didn't, which was why she'd said it.

There were only five pieces of popcorn on his string. She gestured to it. "And you're not finished."

He narrowed his eyes at her.

"I'm not contributing much," he said. "Just holding this needle."

"Holding things seems to be your new specialty."

He harrumphed a little.

"Have you never decorated a Christmas tree before?" Edith seemed appalled at the very idea.

"We decorated one at home last year," her little brother piped in. "I helped."

"We cut out paper snowflakes, and we had cranberries with the popcorn for our garlands, and I got an orange in my stocking. Just like mama did when she was little." Pride emanated from Edith's voice.

Ida found herself holding her breath, praying that Tom wouldn't dismiss the simple pleasures that the girl described. They must seem so trivial to him. Silly even.

He nodded, swallowing. An awkward beat of silence passed before he said, "This will be the very first tree I've decorated."

He glanced at Ida and then away.

Walt claimed Tom was a consummate actor, but she didn't think he was pretending to be uncomfortable. How did one pass into adulthood without having experienced any of the Christmas rituals that made such fond memories?

"You should hang up the first string," Archie said earnestly.

Tom looked skeptically at their string, which had only grown by two kernels. "I'm not sure we'll be finished by the time the tree arrives."

Edith patted his arm. "You can share ours." She pointed at the table where several strands were finished. Julia, Laura, and Grover were working on more.

Tom cleared his throat. "I'm not sure that's a good idea. I'll probably just watch."

"Why?" Archie asked the question with the pure innocence of a four-year-old who'd known only goodness in his life.

If she thought Tom would have an easy, offhand answer, she was mistaken. Some emotion she couldn't name passed over his face.

It was obvious that no one had told the younger children he was a criminal. How they'd missed the shackles at his feet, she couldn't imagine.

If he admitted it to them at that moment, the innocent trust they'd showed by coming to him would be shattered.

She stepped in before he could come up with an answer. "Mr. Tom has some injuries you can't see. More than just his broken arm. He has to stay sitting down most of the time. But I'm sure he'll enjoy watching you hang your garlands on the tree."

Both children accepted this with serious nods, and Tom shot her a relieved look.

"Do you want me to show you how to cut a paper snowflake?" Edith asked.

Tom opened his mouth to answer, but it was her little brother who exclaimed, "Yeah!"

Attention diverted, the two scampered off,

leaving him holding the needle with his sad little strand of popcorn.

"Don't tell them I've never set foot in a schoolroom. Next they'll have me doing sums on a slate."

She didn't look at Tom, though she sensed him watching her. Did he expect her to feel pity for him? It *was* a pity that he hadn't had a real childhood.

She kept her gaze on the children as they tugged on their mother's skirt. Ida couldn't hear their words, but they pointed to where Ida stood beside Tom's chair, and she imagined they wanted Breanna to fetch paper and scissors to teach him how to make snowflakes.

There was no missing the concern in Breanna's expression as she glanced their direction and then back at her children.

Ida watched her try to dissuade the children. She saw the slump of Archie's shoulders and the pout on Edith's lips.

Tom must've seen it too. "I've never hurt anybody." His voice emerged so low she almost didn't hear it.

She didn't say anything, and he glanced up at her. "Your brother probably filled your head with nonsense about all the things I've done."

Walt. He was talking about Walt and the quest he'd undertaken to bring Tom to justice.

She shook her head. "Before the train, I hadn't seen Walt in years. I know he's been after you and your brothers for a long time."

Walt had scarcely written home and never shared details about what he was doing. She'd heard some secondhand accounts and read in the newspapers about robberies and heists the outlaw gang had undertaken.

But at this moment, she couldn't remember reading specifically about Tom's part in the crimes.

"I told you so back at the hideout. I wasn't lying. I was usually the lookout." His voice was still low. "Or the one wrangling the horses. Or checking out the town ahead of time."

She could see that. He was handsome and usually well-groomed, though right now he didn't look it with scruff at his chin and his borrowed clothes too big and rumpled.

"I don't cotton to hurting innocents."

Maybe not, but he was guilty nevertheless. If he stood by while his brothers had hurt and killed people, he was just as responsible. Wasn't he?

He must've seen the stiff way she was holding herself. She forced her shoulders to relax.

He muttered something under his breath, but this time, she didn't catch the words. Maybe something like, *not that it matters.*

Did it matter? He'd said they were friends, but they weren't really. They didn't know anything about each other.

She didn't need a friend like Tom. She needed her courage back.

She excused herself and slipped through the crowd to the kitchen, intending to see if Mama needed more help.

She saw Edith and Archie run back to Tom with paper and a pencil in hand, their excitement spilling over.

For one moment, she saw a flash of vulnerability cross his face.

He glanced up and met her eyes across the room and then cut his eyes away quickly, his expression shuttering.

Seeing his vulnerability made her chest feel tight, but she forced herself to slip into the kitchen.

Tom was going to prison in a few days. Walt seemed sure that he would be convicted.

There was no room for friendship here.

But even as her hands were busy helping Mama with the supper preparations, that moment of vulnerability stuck with her.

She was surrounded by family who loved her.

Tom had no one.

He would never admit to it, but did he need a friend?

Maybe if she could bear his presence, she would be ready to get on a train again and move on with her life.

Then he'd leave.

The question was, could she do it?

CHAPTER 5

Tom had never eaten anything as good as the meal Ida and her mama prepared while the rest of the family trimmed the tree Andrew and the two other teens had dragged into the house. He hadn't been trusted with shears, but the pencil-drawn pictures the two children had drawn at his knee were also hung on the tree.

He didn't know how they fed so many mouths. It seemed as if, like the family members, the food kept coming and coming. Yeasty rolls that melted on his tongue. Ham and green beans and mashed potatoes.

The only black mark on the experience came from sitting next to one of Ida's older brothers. The man seemed determined to jostle Tom's arm at every chance, as if it were some kind of game. Tom knew it wasn't accidental. He was supposed to be reminded on his place here—and the fact that he didn't have one.

The only reason he'd been seated at the table and not on the sofa with some of the other adults was because he couldn't balance a plate on his lap with only one hand.

The meal was wrapping up when one more couple and their ten-year-old son came in through the back door. They were greeted warmly—another brother, apparently—but Tom couldn't help noticing that the wife was missing her right arm.

Not long after the meal, the younger children were put to bed. One or two of the brothers left on foot with their wives and children, but there were still plenty left to keep an eye on Tom, including the tall, broad-shouldered man who'd arrived late in the evening.

The oldest, dark-haired brother that might've been named Oscar set up a checkerboard across the room at a small table between two chairs. The teen boy probably named Leo sat in one of the chairs, expectantly waiting.

The dinner table emptied except for Tom at his end and Andrew at the other. The boy was poring over a book, though he glanced up to check on Tom every time he turned the page.

Wasn't the teen getting bored of his self-appointed task watching Tom's every move? There'd been no opportunity to sneak away, not in the crush of bodies. He wouldn't make it far on foot in the dark, considering the unfamiliar surroundings.

At least, that was what he told himself. Truth was, he'd gotten caught up in watching the dynamics of this family. He'd never experienced anything like it.

Right now, folks were sneaking gifts beneath the tree. Most were wrapped in brown paper and tied with twine.

He was surprised when Ida and the woman with only one arm approached him. Ida's arms were full of things he couldn't identify except for several paintbrushes. Her companion came right over to Tom and began spreading out several sheets of newspaper on the table.

"Do you want me to…?" *Move?*

But Ida was shaking her head.

"You've been sitting like a bump on a log," she said. Was she teasing him? Her manner was different than it had been earlier. Some tension remained, but underneath, she seemed determined. "We need to paint these, and you've been recruited to help."

Ida deposited two unpainted wooden toy tops

on the newspaper in front of him. It began to make sense. Those small pots she was carrying held paint. She laid them out in front of him as well.

He raised his cast, ignoring the pull in his side. "How am I supposed to paint without making a mess?"

It was Ida's companion who answered. "I'm afraid I needed an extra hand, and you've been nominated."

Completely at ease, she waved her left hand— her only hand—before she tucked her skirts beneath her and sat in the chair next to him. She handed him one of the tops and, since she was the first person besides Ida who'd spoken to him in over an hour, he took it without thinking.

"I might not be any good at this," she said, "but we'll give it a try. If you would just hold..."

His gaze went to Ida. Her lips were pressed together, and her eyes danced. She was as pretty as a hothouse rose, and for a moment he was struck dumb. He quickly recovered. "You want me to hold it."

Ida couldn't contain the small smile that broke free. "I'm afraid so."

His smile trailed her as she disappeared into the kitchen, leaving him with a woman he hadn't been introduced to.

"And you are...? I'm sorry, there are a lot of names to remember—"

"And probably half of them haven't introduced themselves to you," she finished. Her gaze was steady as it rested on him momentarily. "I'm Daisy. Ricky's wife."

She said that as if it explained everything. Ricky must be the man she'd arrived with.

She adjusted the top so it was tilted more toward her. Her nose wrinkled slightly as she considered it before picking up a paintbrush.

"And who are we painting these toys for?"

It was Ida who answered his question as she returned to the table. This time her hands were full of... corn husks? "Breanna's surprise visit means there won't be enough gifts under the tree. We all want to spoil Edith and Archie just as much as the other children."

It was a thoughtful gesture. He'd always known other folks were different from his family. He'd watched a mother and her two small children once when he was supposed to be casing a bank. He'd seen the older of two little boys spill his sandwich into the street.

Tom would've been slapped across the face and gone hungry for that transgression.

But the young mother had given her own sandwich to the boy.

Tom could still remember the shock he'd felt. Watching the mother and her sons had felt like make-believe. A made up story from a fairytale book.

Ida's family made him feel the same way. This couldn't possibly be real.

Daisy swept her paintbrush across the surface of the top, spreading on deep blue paint that reminded him of a sky just after the sunset.

"I remember when Chester was small," she said, fondness in her voice. "He was always in desperate need of new socks. He could wear out a new pair in a week. Still can." There was affection in her voice. "His father and I would always put an extra pair beneath the tree, but he never seemed to even notice them, always more drawn to toys like this."

"I was the same way," Ida said.

She had her attention fully fixed on the corn husks she was bending and twisting. What was she making?

He didn't have anything to contribute to their conversation, and his eyes fell to the newspaper flat on the table. He squinted at the small print. Was that his name?

He was distracted by the article until Daisy said, "They can be a little overwhelming at first."

Was she...? She was talking to him.

"Big families take some getting used to." She was making conversation as if he were a guest here. Surely she'd noticed the chains around his legs. But she was acting as if he were an acquaintance.

"And ours is bigger than most," Ida murmured.

What was this? He didn't understand why they were being friendly toward him. But he wasn't going to squander the opportunity to learn what he could.

"Your father and mother don't seem old enough to have all these kids. Not everyone here is related, are they?" It had been bugging him all evening.

"It's quite the story," Daisy said.

"My papa was fired from his job and run out of Philadelphia when Breanna was a newborn," Ida explained. "He moved west. On the way, he met up with a couple of boys who were in trouble and had been abandoned. He adopted them."

"How many boys?" he asked.

"Six."

His shock must've shown on his face because she laughed.

Andrew, sitting at the end of the table, looked up sharply.

Daisy motioned for Tom to turn the top around. It was awkward to twist his wrist, but he did, presenting her with the unpainted side.

Daisy's husband, who had dirty blond hair and gray eyes, came to stand behind her chair, resting his hands on its back. He was unsmiling.

"We were a rough and tumble bunch back then," the man said. "I don't know how Pa stood to be around us."

"Only back then?" Daisy teased. She sent an expressive glance toward the man and boy arguing over the chess match. "The last time we came for Christmas, you got into a wrestling match with Oscar and broke one of your mother's end tables. I had to put ointment on your knuckles."

"And you kissed them better." He smiled a private smile just for his wife, who looked over her shoulder adoringly at him.

Tom was still stuck on what Ida had said earlier. "Your father adopted six boys," he said to her. "Of his own volition?"

"All before he met my mother," she said with a quicksilver grin. "Of course, Oscar and Maxwell were out of the house before Andrew was born, so not all ten of us children have lived here at the same time."

He shook his head, still not quite able to believe

it. It sounded crazy.

Daisy took the top from him, its base painted blue. She seemed to have trouble finding a way to set it down so that the paint wouldn't smear, and her husband bent over her shoulder to try and help figure out a way to balance it.

Tom watched Ida, who had gone back to making her dolls. "Why would your father do that?"

It must've been difficult to feed all of those mouths. To be on his own, no wife to help, trying to eke a living out of the land.

Ida's expression was soft. "Because they needed him."

He scanned the words on the newspaper beneath his hands, only halfway taking them in.

"All of us came from rough situations," Ricky said. The look he turned on Tom was less than friendly. "Pa made choices that turned his choices around, and then he helped us all do the same. Maybe things could've ended worse, but even when it was hard, Pa chose right."

The words were clearly meant as an attack on Tom. *Choices. Their Pa chose right.*

And Tom hadn't. That was the clear subtext. He met the other man's stare squarely. "Not everyone has the freedom to make those kinds of decisions."

Tom pushed up from the table. He was done

there.

———

IDA FOLLOWED TOM, with his awkward shuffling gait, down the hall.

She heard movement behind her and knew that at least one of her brothers was following.

Tom stopped in the middle of the hallway, looking between the multiple doors. No one had shown him to his room yet.

"You're on the left." There were two doors on the left. He reached for the first, and she said, "The other one."

"Goodnight," he muttered before he pushed in through the door. He was so slow that it was no effort at all to follow him in.

"Ida," her brother warned. It was Oscar, not Ricky, like she'd thought. But a glance past her oldest brother and she saw Ricky hovering just behind.

She didn't need to be coddled. "I need to check his wound. Maxwell can do it tomorrow, but for tonight it'll have to be me. I'll leave the door open." Maxwell had gone home earlier because Hattie wasn't feeling well.

Oscar looked uncertain, and Ricky bunched up

beside him.

"He's incapacitated. He can barely move. I'll leave the door open," she repeated. And her brothers had better stay on the other side of it.

Inside the bedroom, Tom looked at the bed with its quilted cover. Or maybe he was eyeing the window. After years of the house settling, that one stuck. He would never get it open with one hand, not without raising enough noise to wake the entire house. Mama had probably put him in this room for that reason.

"I'd like to go to bed now." He didn't look at her.

She knew he'd heard her speak to her brother. "After I've checked your bandage."

He turned toward her and lifted his shirt with his good hand, his movements quick and almost violent. But she wasn't frightened of him. He'd had opportunities to take advantage, when she was trapped with him and the other outlaws. He hadn't taken them then, and her brothers were nearby now.

She would rather he were lying down, but she didn't argue, only stepped closer. His skin was warm under her fingertips. "What happened back there?"

He shook his head, his chin set at a stubborn angle.

She'd heard Ricky's words and how Tom had responded. *Not everyone has the freedom to make those kind of decisions.*

Had the conversation really upset him enough to stomp off? Ricky hadn't been particularly kind, but with all they'd been through, she'd never seen Tom have an emotional reaction like that. Not even when he'd first been in Walt's custody. Tom had seemed relaxed then, even bored.

Ricky's words couldn't have set him off so badly that his self-control slipped.

"How tender is it?" she asked, pressing on his side around the outer edges of the bandage.

"Ow!" He twisted slightly and then must've tweaked his ribs because he inhaled sharply. "Of course it's still tender if you jab it like that!"

She looked up at him in the darkened room— darkened because she hadn't thought to grab a candle—and saw the muscle jumping in his cheek.

"If you're in pain, I need to know."

His eyes glittered down at her before he backed away from her touch and paced toward the window. He ran one hand through his hair.

She had never seen him agitated like this. "What's going on?"

"Is that newspaper recent? The one you put out on the table."

The newspaper? What did the newspaper have to do with anything? "I think it was from yesterday. Why?"

He leaned against the wall. "It had our names in it. It was some kind of article about how you'd been rescued and me captured."

"I don't understand."

"My brothers will see it." He spat the words.

"It's the local paper," she said. "From town."

"So it is, but your big-shot brother-in-law is here. I heard someone say he's in the newspaper business. What's to keep him from running the story in his big Boston newspaper? Or anywhere else. Everyone wants to print stories about the Seymour gang. And if it gets printed more widely? My brothers will be coming here. Sooner rather than later."

"You already said they were coming." Her voice was shaking now.

His face went carefully blank. "I'm sure they are."

Was he? Or had he said it only to make her afraid? Walt was right. Tom had manipulated her back at the jailhouse. Had he wanted to end up here, at her parents' home?

He must've seen her anger bubbling up. He stepped closer to her. She waved him off, as if that would stop him. "You said—"

"What I said was true. If they know I'm alive, they'll come for me. They think we know where the gold is, remember?"

Because he'd told them that *she* knew where the loot was.

She began to tremble and started to step away, but he rested his good hand on her wrist and held fast.

"I thought we were friends," she hissed. She heard rustling in the hallway and remembered her brothers were just outside.

His teeth flashed in the dim light. "I don't know if I could ever be friends with you."

She saw his intentions when he dipped his head toward her. He was going to kiss her. All she had to do was take one step back. Or call out for her brothers.

But the combination of all of it—her fear, the snatches of vulnerability she'd seen in him today, his warmth… She moved toward him instead of away. His lips covered hers in a kiss that was both tender and desperate.

What was she doing? Her thoughts finally caught up to her actions, and she took a step back. His eyes were glittering in the dimness.

She suddenly had to escape.

CHAPTER 6

The next morning, Ida's heart pounded as she heard the clink of Tom's chains on the back stoop. She stood at the kitchen counter, knowing he'd come inside at any moment. She pressed her hands to her cheeks but then thought better of it and whipped them down beside her as the back door opened.

He glanced up and caught sight of her, his eyes softening and going warm in a way that made her cheeks burn.

She should never have kissed him.

"Morning," he said, his voice gravelly with sleep.

"Good morning."

He sent a disgruntled look over his shoulder. "Your brother was kind enough to show me the way to the outhouse." The edge to his voice said he found it anything other than kind.

She poured two cups of coffee and handed one to Tom and the other to Edgar, who followed him inside. Edgar and Fran and their two children lived in a cabin just on the other side of the creek. Had he been on watch? The thought was both comforting and frightening.

Tom's jaw had darkened even more with unshaved whiskers, making him look disreputable. As he should.

"You're up early," he said after his first sip.

It was early. The shadows were long and the sun was just beginning to peek over the horizon.

"It's Christmas."

He shrugged and sent her a questioning look.

She went back to stuffing the turkey. "The children will be up any minute." And once Christmas had come and gone, she would have to make some decisions about her future. Yesterday, Maxwell had asked her about her plans, and she hadn't had an answer for him. "There's a lot of preparation for the noon meal." She focused on Edgar. "Mama's fiddling with the tree."

Her brother didn't smile, but that wasn't unusual. Edgar was never fully awake until he'd had at least two cups of coffee. He stood in the living room doorway, looking at Mama.

Tom took a couple of shuffling steps toward her. "Anything I can help with? I'm getting good at holding onto stuff."

She didn't know whether he had meant it that way, but his words made her think of how his hand had curled around her waist for those brief moments the night before.

Her cheeks burned again.

His eyes smiled even though his lips didn't so much as twitch.

"No, thank you." She switched her attention back to the bird in front of her. She'd need to get the turkey in the oven soon or lunch would be late.

"You're good at all this stuff." He motioned to the kitchen around them. "All the candy last night and supper, too. Homemaking stuff."

"I've been helping Mama in the kitchen since I was little."

"You'll make a fine wife someday."

She didn't know what he was getting at and just shook her head. "That's a ways off," she said. "I have aspirations." He didn't need to know she was afraid to put any ideas into motion.

"What kinda aspirations?"

"Libby and I had planned on becoming traveling

nurses." She shrugged and smiled a little. "I don't know whether her ambitions will change now that there's something happening between her and Walt. There are a lot of communities without doctors. A lot of people I could help."

He watched her thoughtfully. "That's very noble of you."

What would his future hold? Would he really go to prison, like Walt thought? How long would he serve? The unanswered questions made her stomach feel sick.

Edgar had apparently been summoned by Mama, because he sent a glance over his shoulder and moved slowly into the living room.

"What would you do?" she asked tentatively, "if you weren't—" That wasn't quite right. "If you were free to do what you wanted."

His eyes glittered in a way that made him seem dangerous, but when she blinked, he was smiling and sipping his coffee.

"If I were a different man," he said slowly, "I would probably travel far away from here. Start over in a place where nobody knew the name Seymour."

"But what would you do? Try your hand at farming? Get a job in a factory? Write a novel?"

"Farming seems like a thankless occupation. You

toil and toil and the weather can make you destitute in one season. No offense intended. Your father's got a fine spread." He looked out the window. "I don't have any experience with factories or putting pen to paper. Maybe I'll do something completely different. Find a ship. Sail the world."

That sounded like a fantasy.

Focused on her task, she asked in as casual a voice as she could muster, "And if you were a free man? Would you find a wife? Start a family?"

"You applying for the job?"

"Be serious."

Emotion flickered through his eyes before his expression closed off. "I don't know."

"Never really thought about it before?"

He sipped his coffee again, staying silent.

Edgar would be back soon. Or another of her brothers. She and Tom wouldn't be alone for much longer. "About last night..." she started.

His gaze returned to her, so intent that something tumbled in her stomach.

"We shouldn't have done that."

He shook his head. "I disagree."

"It will only muddle things," she said, "in our friendship."

Did he realize what she was offering him? He was the one who'd used the word *friends* first. He'd said it more than once, though she knew he'd done it in the beginning to get under her skin.

But she was offering him a real friendship.

That was all it could be. Nothing more. He started to answer, but before he could, Mama bustled into the kitchen.

———

Tom had no further chance to talk with Ida because every small child in the house seemed to wake at the same time.

Ida finished whatever she was doing with the large turkey and lugged it over to the oven and slid it over the fire.

When she moved into the living room, Tom followed her. Her brother's sharp stare followed Tom.

Ida hugged each of her nieces and nephews and then huddled with them in front of the tree, whispering and pointing at the piles of gifts beneath.

He stood back even though what he wanted to do was pull Ida aside and demand answers. Was she sincere? Did she really want to be friends? What did that mean?

Would she help him—? No. No matter how she might claim to be his friend, her moral compass was too strong for her to even think about helping him escape his shackles.

He'd already wasted one chance that morning. He'd slipped out of the house without anyone knowing and been halfway to the outhouse—his mind still halfway in dreamland, remembering the feel of Ida's lips against his—when he'd realized he was alone.

Edgar had caught up to him before he'd reached the tiny shack, before he could even think which way to go. If he'd been more aware of his surroundings, could he have slipped away into the darkness?

Edgar hadn't wasted any time in telling him, "My brothers and I know every nook and cranny on this land. There's nowhere you could hide that we wouldn't find you."

Maybe so.

But if Tom saw his chance, he was taking it. He couldn't just sit there and wait for Walt to return and escort him to prison.

It wasn't long before movement came from down the hall. Soon enough, the room was full. The children sat in front of the tree ripping open packages while the teens and adults watched indulgently.

The little boy gasped over the top that Tom had helped paint. If you could call what he'd done "helping."

The adults were handed gifts too.

He watched Ida's mother open a fine shawl and send Ida a teary smile. Seeing it made him wonder what had happened to the knitting she'd had with her on the train.

There was a hushed, "You shouldn't have," from one of the wives closest to him. He missed whatever gift shouldn't have been given.

And then he was rendered speechless when Edith made her way through discarded paper and the teens lounging on the floor to press a brown-wrapped package into his hands.

A gift—for him?

He turned the package over in his good hand. There were no markings on it. Only a small bit of twine that held it together.

He looked up, intending to protest that this couldn't be for him, but the girl had already returned to her pile of treasures. His gaze clashed with Ida's as she watched him from across the room.

He raised his brows. *You?* he mouthed.

She nodded minutely.

Something hot and uncomfortable lodged in his chest and he stared down at the package. This had to be a sign that she was serious about a real friendship with him.

But it was also... more. He couldn't remember a

time that his brothers had given him a gift. Or anyone, for that matter.

He was still planning to get out of there as soon as he could. This might be the last gift he ever received. Once he opened it, it would be done.

When he glanced up again, Ida was still watching. She must've seen his struggle because she smiled wryly. *It's not much*, she mouthed to him.

Maybe not to her...

He could feel his heartbeat in the lobes of his ears as he looked down at the package again. He couldn't bear the anticipation any longer. His fingers felt clumsy as the knot in the twine fell away. The paper folded back, crackling under his fingers, and he lifted out a knitted scarf. A handmade scarf in bright red yarn. He fingered it, noticing the workmanship. It wasn't a simple design. Somehow she'd patterned it into diamonds. She'd obviously spent some time on this. Was it a mistake? What if he had misunderstood her, and this was meant to be a gift for someone else, someone she cared about?

When he glanced up, Andrew was glaring at him, as usual. Ida's father was watching his daughter, an expression on his face that Tom couldn't read. Another brother was watching Tom as well—maybe his name was Davy?

But when his eyes connected with Ida's again, it was the jolt of connection that shocked him.

Her gaze was warm and open.

He had to swallow the sudden hot knot of emotion in his throat.

Thank you. He flipped the scarf over his shoulders so that it hung down on both sides of his neck.

She nodded, a smile appearing that was meant for him alone. She was soon distracted by one of the teen girls sitting at her side.

Ida obviously didn't care that her brothers had seen Tom receive her gift or that they would know she was the one who'd given it.

Her warmth and joy filled him even across the room.

Friends.

Had he ever had a real friend? Someone who hadn't wanted something from him? Someone he hadn't used?

He couldn't think of one.

If he allowed himself to get close to her, would he still be able to walk away?

CHAPTER 7

Ida was putting away the last dish after helping clean up from the noon meal when Edgar found her. He held her coat and scarf in one hand and nodded toward the back door. "Would you take a walk with me?"

"Of course." She knew he must want to talk about Tom. She had nothing to say, but the concern on her brother's face touched her. They'd never been as close as she was with Walt, but she knew Edgar was looking out for her.

It was worse than she'd expected. Outside, Andrew, Matty, Oscar, and Seb were waiting at the bottom of the porch steps. Wonderful.

The cold bit her cheeks as she tucked her scarf around her neck and secured it in her coat, buttoning the last button over it.

Apprehension tightened her gut, but she joined them anyway.

"I'm the lucky one today, aren't I? To get all this special attention from my brothers?" It was on the tip of her tongue to ask who was watching Tom, but she decided against it. No use in antagonizing them.

"Where should we walk to?" she asked brightly.

Edgar shrugged, but Oscar jerked his chin to gesture west. Her brothers grouped around her in a loose bundle when she set out at a brisk stride, her boots crunching through the hardened top layer of snow.

Taking a deep breath of frosty air, she let her eyes sweep the snow covered horizon. The cold snap they'd endured the past few days meant the snow from three days ago hadn't melted off yet, and it made for a pretty picture.

Who would be the first to speak? Perhaps Oscar? He was the oldest. Or Matty, the sheriff's deputy.

She knew what they were doing. Interfering. She had given Tom that scarf this morning, and her brothers didn't like it. She'd witnessed times like this before. When one member of the family needed a little nudge, the brothers took it upon their nosy selves to do the nudging. Or pushing, as might be the case.

But they were awfully quiet, and her ears and

nose were getting cold. She rubbed her mittened hands together. "Who shall go first?"

"Ida." It was Andrew.

What could the youngest of all her brothers have to say? He'd barely begun to experience life away from the family homestead.

"You're going to tell me that Tom is dangerous. I already know that."

I don't cotton to hurting innocents. Tom had told her that the day before. At the time, she hadn't been sure she could believe him. But today, something had changed between them.

Even so, it didn't mean he wasn't dangerous in other ways. She remembered the flash of his eyes just before he'd leaned in and kissed her.

"We don't want to see you get hurt." Now Oscar spoke, his voice compassionate and caring, like the father he'd become.

"I've already been hurt," she snapped. Her feet stomped the next few steps. "And threatened, chased down and nearly fallen to my death. I survived."

Beside her, Edgar reached out to put his arm around her.

She stepped to the side, avoiding his touch.

His arm fell back to the side. "We're thankful you're all right. But I've seen the way you look at him, and—"

"The way I look at him?" She threw her hands up, laughing a little. "What about the way you all look at him? You've all accepted Walt's grudge as truth. It seems you're forgetting he saved my life."

"You saved his life," Seb said. Other than Walt, Seb was the closest brother to her in age. She'd noticed that over the past twenty-four hours, he had stayed away from Tom completely. And now he wanted to interfere?

She and Libby had saved Tom's life out in the wilderness when the gunshot wound he'd received had gotten infected and they'd been forced to perform surgery. He'd saved hers when the horse had bolted over the side of that cliff.

They'd saved each other.

"Sometimes, when you go through a dangerous situation like that together, you catch feelings." Seb was serious. Almost sorrowful.

"I don't have feelings for him. The man needs a friend. In two days' time, Walt is going to take him straight to prison. That would be frightening enough for one of us. We've got our whole family surrounding us. Tom has no one."

She whirled and pushed past Matty and Davy, who'd been walking closest behind her. It was Christmas, and she didn't want to argue.

"I thought maybe you'd understand," she sent the

words toward Seb as a parting shot over her shoulder. Her brother had left the family for a time. He'd fallen in with the wrong crowd in Colorado before he'd nearly died and come to his senses.

He called after her. "If you think he's got your best interests at heart, you're wrong. Somebody like that doesn't change."

"You did."

The pounding of hoofbeats had the men's heads whipping towards the sound. For one wild moment, Ida wondered if Tom had gotten loose of his chains and somehow made it out to the barn to steal a horse. She instantly recognized it for the silly thought it was. If he'd gotten loose, why would he ride directly toward the people who wanted to keep him contained?

It was Breanna on the horse's back, wrapped in a coat and scarf.

She reined in nearby.

"Should you be riding in your condition?" Oscar strode toward her.

Breanna grinned. "It didn't seem to hurt when I was pregnant with Edith or Archie."

She took in Ida, now standing with her arms crossed, and shook her head. "I told the lot of you to leave it be."

She beckoned to Ida, who strode the last few

steps to her and grabbed Breanna's outstretched hand. She used Breanna's booted foot in the stirrup as a step, and her sister tugged her up into the saddle behind her.

A moment later, Breanna was riding the horse into a canter not toward the house but toward the pasture. Breanna loved to race. She didn't seem to know how to ride slowly.

The rushing air against Ida's face made her shiver.

Breanna must've felt it. "We won't ride for long," she said over her shoulder. "I've missed being home and wanted to see how the land has changed."

Ida was grateful for both the interruption and for her sister's silence. They followed the creek until she turned the animal to cross behind a gully, which put them on top of the hill where they could look down over the homestead. From this distance, it seemed so peaceful. Smoke rose from the chimney of the old house, from Oscar and Sarah's place on one side of the valley and from Edgar and Fran's on the other.

The peacefulness of the view was nothing like the turmoil that Ida had felt those last few moments with her brothers. Why couldn't they try to understand?

"They can be so overprotective sometimes, can't they?" Breanna asked.

"Sometimes it feels like they think I don't have a brain at all," Ida said.

"When it's really the lot of them who need to put their brains together to have one original thought."

Ida smiled at that, though it faded too quickly. "They didn't say anything I haven't said to myself."

Breanna squeezed Ida's knee. "You're a smart girl. Whatever happens, you know the family is here for you."

She did know that. And she was thankful for it.

She was safe here. Not so long ago, she'd felt stifled, needing to stretch her wings.

Now she was afraid to leave.

Breanna knew, somehow. Her hand remained on Ida's knee, a comforting touch.

Obviously Ida had no future with Tom, not even friendship, past the next two days. But he had no one else. Why shouldn't she be his friend? Her brothers were worried over nothing.

Her eyes scanned further afield. Davy and Rose's cabin was just over the horizon there. And Matty and Catherine's place was tucked in that copse of trees where the trees met the foothills.

This land told the story of their family. It was their legacy and would provide for their children and their children's children. She'd belonged here since her birth, and she always would, just like the land called to Breanna, even though she'd moved away.

Tom didn't have this. His family legacy was a nightmare.

If she could share this with him, even for a day or two, she would.

Her brothers would simply have to accept it.

———

TOM WASN'T such a dunce that he didn't notice when Ida and her brothers disappeared.

He couldn't exactly go after them to find out what they wanted.

But when her brothers, looking disgruntled, returned to the house without her, it took everything in him not to demand to know where she was.

And then she burst into the house, her cheeks and nose pink from the cold. Breanna was with her, and they were laughing at some private joke, and all was right in the world again.

He'd planned to tell someone about the newspaper article. Maybe Matty. But her brothers steered clear of him. And the two little kids, Archie and Edith, stuck close. He didn't want to say anything in front of the children, so he swallowed the notion.

Breanna tugged her husband down the hallway, and they disappeared into one of the bedrooms. Several of the brothers left. Jonas and Penny excused themselves to make a quick visit to one of their neighbors.

And suddenly, the room was much quieter.

Ida brought him a cup of coffee and laid her hand on his shoulder briefly and then was drawn into a game of marbles with her niece and nephew.

He watched her, amazed at how quickly her smiles came, how comfortable she was with the two children.

What if...?

What would it take to have someone like her in his life?

He didn't look up when he sensed someone hovering. Not until the person approached him directly. He looked up to see one of Ida's brothers, this one on the younger side. He was holding a sleeping toddler against his shoulder.

"I'm Seb."

Tom nodded. Seb. Out of all of Ida's relatives, Seb had stayed the farthest from him since the family had congregated the night before.

"You play checkers?" Seb jerked his head toward the board now set up at the end of the dinner table.

Tom wondered what the man's angle was. "It's been a while, but all right."

As he shuffled across the room behind Seb, Breanna's husband Adam returned from their bedroom, a newspaper in hand, and installed himself on the sofa near the fire to read it.

Ida glanced at Tom but didn't abandon her game with the children.

Tom sat in the same seat he'd occupied the night before. His opponent had given him the black checkers. Seb still held that little girl against his shoulder, fast asleep.

Both Seb and Tom had made three moves each when the back door opened and closed.

"Halloo the house," a male voice called.

Every eye in the room turned to the kitchen doorway where a man with a tin star on his chest appeared. This was the deputy who had, with Matty, escorted Tom to the homestead.

His sharp gaze landed on Tom first, then swung to Seb, taking in the checkerboard between them. If anything, his gaze hardened when it landed on Seb, who turned to face the board without greeting him.

Ida pushed up off the floor, brushing out her

skirt, while Breanna's husband went back to his paper.

Belatedly, the deputy swept his hat off his head. "Thought I'd stop by and wish you happy Christmas."

More like he thought he should check on the prisoner.

Tom's lips twisted.

Ida's gaze glanced off Seb, her brow furrowing for a moment before smoothing again. She smiled at the deputy as she neared. "Mama and Papa have gone visiting with Oscar and Sarah. You must be in need of warming. Let me fix you a cup of coffee."

"I'd like that." His head tilted toward her, and he smiled as she passed by him. Before he followed her into the kitchen, his eyes cut to Tom and Seb again.

"It's your move," Seb said.

Tom blinked and attempted to refocus. He'd had a strategy in mind before the interruption, but now his brain was buzzing with trying to hear what Ida was saying in the kitchen.

The man across from him spoke, and Ida's murmur was lost. "My folks don't talk about it, but I was in a bad place for a couple years. Like you."

Tom kept his eyes on the checkerboard as the other man jumped one of his checkers and removed it from the board. "You don't say," he drawled.

"I had some help, but I was able to make things right, and my family forgave me. I came back home."

Tom could guess why Seb was telling him this. Ida's family was full of do-gooders. They wanted to make him into one of them.

Maybe this brother thought he could help Tom.

But experience had taught him that the only person who could get him out of this was himself.

They played several more moves without speaking. Seb was sharp, Tom would give him that. He'd taken all but two of Tom's checkers. One of them was backed into a corner, and if he moved the piece, it would be taken.

Seb made two more moves before they reached a stalemate. Seb shifted the girl on his shoulder.

If Tom moved his only free checker forward, Seb followed him. If he moved it back, Seb followed that too.

So Tom gave up. He put his hand in his lap and looked across the table to the other man. "I guess that's it."

Seb's expression was serious. Not angry or suspicious, like the looks Tom had been receiving since his arrival. He looked almost... earnest. "Sometimes a man gets backed into a corner and doesn't know which way to turn."

Ida's lilting laugh filtered in from the other

room, and Tom's attention darted to the kitchen doorway.

Seb missed nothing.

Something sour and ugly settled in Tom's stomach. He'd seen the deputy chatting with Ida on the porch on Christmas Eve. Did she fancy the man?

No. It was Tom she'd kissed.

Though she'd said it had been a mistake.

Seb reset the checkerboard and took the first move, gesturing for Tom to play again.

He wanted to get up and march into the kitchen and demand Ida talk to *him*. Laugh with *him*.

But he pushed a checker across the board.

"My wife Emma changed me," Seb said.

Tom made himself refocus on the conversation.

"When I was making bad decisions and couldn't get my life in order, she had faith in me. She was probably the only one who did."

Was he comparing his saint of a wife to Ida? Saying Ida was the only one who saw anything good in Tom?

"Sometimes knowing a good woman is behind him is enough to put a man on the straight and narrow."

Mentally, Tom could see the next two moves play out. His moves were limited by the other man's pieces, and the game was already won.

Not by him.

The deputy came back into the room, Ida hovering in the doorway behind him. His eyes narrowed on Seb again at the table. This time, Tom noticed a fine tension ratchet up Seb's shoulders. Was there a problem between the two men? Did it go back to that dark time in Seb's life that he was talking about?

The deputy gave Tom one more sharp glance, said goodbye to Ida, and walked out.

Tom's stomach still felt leaden. Was this jealousy? He didn't much like the ugly feeling streaking through him.

"I believe any man can be redeemed," Seb said. The words were for Tom's ears only, spoken low. "I was."

Tom stared at him. "And if he doesn't need redeeming?"

He held Tom's stare without speaking. And then the young child on his shoulder murmured and began to rouse. Seb walked away, and Tom was left to his thoughts.

He saw the anger and concern from Ida's family.

She'd been hurt. He *was* sorry for that. She didn't deserve what happened to her. Neither did anyone else he and his brothers had stolen from.

He'd never cared before. Never felt he'd needed to make reparations.

But the more time he spent with Ida's family, the more that uncomfortable feeling in his chest grew.

It still didn't mean he needed redeeming.

CHAPTER 8

I da felt sure Tom was up to something.

He'd been quiet and contemplative since Deputy Fletcher had gone. Soon after, Mama and Papa had returned from visiting.

All of the aunts and uncles and nieces and nephews converged again and ate an informal dinner of leftovers and cold meats and cheese.

Matty and Catherine's son, Harvey, had challenged his uncle Ricky, the reigning champion of marbles, to a game. That had resulted in another challenge and soon, chairs were shoved aside to free up more floor space and both children and adults were engaged in three different matches.

Ida was still miffed with her brothers for their meddling conversation in the cold. But she was working on forgiving them. She knew they meant well.

Plus, she beat Oscar after taking his best shooter, so she was feeling a smidge smug.

Edith teamed up with Tom, who had pled that he was unable to play because of his injured hand. That hadn't stopped him from whispering strategy in her ear, telling her which marbles to shoot for. Working as a team, they beat Leo, Oscar's oldest son.

Tom had looked flabbergasted when Edith had thrown her arms around his neck, cackling gleefully at the win.

And he was still wearing the scarf she'd given him, draped over his shoulders, though he had to be warm in the house, what with all those bodies.

As other challengers took their places, Tom moved to a chair partway behind the sofa, where only his head and shoulders were in sight. Edith and Archie joined him, only the tops of their heads visible. The three held a whispered conversation.

Ida had been drawn into a game herself and couldn't tell what Tom and the two little rascals were up to, but there were plenty of adults watching, so it couldn't be anything nefarious.

Archie ran into the kitchen and then back to Tom, hands hidden behind his back as he moved through the busy room. What did Tom have the child fetch for him?

Tom disappeared down the hall—to his bedroom?—but quickly returned.

Ida was forced to focus on the game when she lost one of her shooters. She only happened to look up at the same moment that Edgar, who was playing in the game farthest across the room, let out a roar.

Tom's head snapped up, his eyes a little wild.

"That's cheating," Edgar snapped, the words clear and loud above the hubbub.

"No, you're cheating!" Oscar argued.

Tom had gone tense, one hand gripping the sofa back. His knuckles were white.

And then Mama chided the boys, and Leo laughed, and the tension was broken.

Ida's gaze flicked back to Tom, who was saying something to Archie as if nothing had happened. Had she imagined his tension?

She was still thinking of those scant seconds an hour later as families began to disburse and children were put to bed. She was gathering up several coffee tins that had been left around the room when Tom approached, shackles rattling against the floor.

"I thought I'd retire early," he said.

At least three pairs of suspicious eyes landed on him.

"I'm having some pain in my side." He winked at her. "You'd better come in and check my bandage."

Twenty-year-old Velma was the nearest person in the room and must've seen his wink because she muffled a giggle behind one hand.

Ida was conscious of Seb's stare from across the room. *Someone like that won't change.*

Tom was joshing around. That wink said everything. Should she go with him?

A beat passed before he lowered his voice, levity fading from his expression. "Please. Just for a moment."

She nodded and detoured to the kitchen to deposit the coffee tins before following him to the bedroom. She'd brought a small lamp this time and set it on a table against the wall. Again, she was careful to leave the door propped open.

He'd gone to the bed and removed his scarf. She saw him run one finger along a fold of the fabric before he looked up at her.

She stayed just inside the door, several feet away, and put her hands on her hips. "All right, where is this pain?"

He put one hand over his heart. "Right here. At the thought of never seeing you again after tomorrow."

She rolled her eyes, but that only made his grin spread.

"Be serious. Are you in real pain?"

He was still smiling, but something shifted behind his eyes. "Why do you think I'm not telling the truth?"

When she didn't answer, his smile grew wry. He beckoned her closer, and she realized his other hand was half-hidden behind his back. What was he up to?

Footsteps and voices grew and then faded as Breanna took her children down the hall. Tom's gaze shifted behind Ida briefly.

She didn't turn to see how many of her brothers had crowded out there to listen. Her earlier irritation returned.

"This is for you." Tom revealed what he'd been hiding, though she couldn't see from so far across the room.

He took a step forward, and so did she, and they met in the middle of the room. In the palm of his hand he held a small piece of cardboard, crudely cut into an oval. Strings had been attached on either side. A flying bird had been drawn in pencil on the cardboard.

She took it from his hand, her fingertips

brushing his palm. "Is this what you and the children were working on so covertly?"

"Nothing's covert when those two are involved, I think. It's a thaumatrope."

So it was. She flipped it to see the other side and glimpsed the birdcage.

"I wanted to give you something, even if it couldn't be much."

His dramatics were easily written off, but the openness in his expression made her pulse pound in her cheeks.

"Why?" she asked.

His eyes cut back to her, dark and serious. "Because no one's ever given me a gift before."

No one? How could that be?

"Thank you," he whispered.

Had he scooted closer, or had she? Suddenly, all the air seemed to have been sucked from the room as she realized how little space was between them.

"Tom." Her protest was weakly spoken, and he didn't move back, but he also didn't reach for her.

"You are the real gift," he said. "I don't want to walk away from you. I wish we had more time." He glanced to the side and she saw the muscles in his throat move.

"Maybe—" *We could write to each other while you're in prison.*

She caught a small breath. "Maybe if you ask Walt, he can help you." Help Tom escape? Not likely. But surely there had to be some way her brother could assist. Could he ask the judge for leniency? Would he?

She couldn't imagine Walt even considering it.

A hardness glittered in Tom's eyes. "I don't think so."

She started to say more, but she lost the words when he stepped even closer. "I don't want to talk about your brother. I want this moment..."

He reached for her, and she moved toward him, closing the last few inches between them.

He kissed her, his hand cupping the back of her head.

Stay. She tried to convey the impossible wish in the press of her lips.

And then someone shuffled their feet out in the hallway, and she jumped away from Tom.

The wry twist of his lips said he understood, even as shadows danced in his eyes.

She hadn't known how to feel about this man. Was he the greedy thief who believed himself above the law? The robber who her brothers said would never change?

Or was he the kind, gentle soul who played with children and drew birds and cages to give a simple gift? The man who'd protected her from his outlaw brothers and even risked his life to save hers?

One of those personas was a lie. She'd been convinced—by her brothers, by her own fears, perhaps—that the kindness was the lie, the greed and arrogance the real man. But the more she knew Tom, the more she realized the truth.

He'd been caught up in something he couldn't control. Raised by bandits for brothers, he'd never known anything else. Still, he'd somehow turned out to be so much better than them.

In this moment, she knew who Tom was. No matter what her brothers thought. No matter what the law said. No matter, any of it.

He was a good man. Maybe he'd never had the opportunity to show it. Maybe he'd never known what that should look like. But deep down, he craved the opportunity to choose good.

She wanted this moment with Tom, and a host of other moments after this

But their time was running out.

———

Tom woke in the dark of night with a feeling of dread. His heart was pounding. He rolled over in bed, the last few moments of his nightmare playing behind his eyes.

He didn't usually remember his dreams, but this one was so vivid that it felt real.

In his dream, he'd relived those moments right after Ralphie had died. But instead of believing the white lie Ida had told about knowing the location of the loot, Hector and Tristan had shot her.

Just like that.

There'd been a jagged moment of time lapse, and the dream had jumped to Tom holding her in his arms as her life seeped away in a crimson stain on the ground.

Even as he blinked against the darkness of the bedroom, he could feel the stickiness of her blood on his hands. He could smell the metallic scent of it. He couldn't stop his brain from replaying the horrific dream moments as the light faded from her eyes.

His subconscious was trying to tell him that his brothers were coming. That was all it was.

He knew better than anyone else that his time was short. He needed to make his escape. He needed to get away before they came for him.

He loathed the thought of leaving Ida unprotected, but she had her family to watch out for her, didn't she? Eight older brothers and a protective father all on alert.

He shifted in the bed, his side paining. He didn't bother closing his eyes, though it was dark enough that he could barely make out the outline of the dresser a few feet away. He wouldn't soon forget the dream images of Ida dying in his arms.

If he had some light, he could read the book he'd borrowed from the living room. The Bible was worn, pages bent and marked up. He could light the lamp, but he didn't want anyone thinking he was trying to escape if they saw it shining under the door.

It was a long time until dawn. He was left with too much time to think.

The conversation with Seb repeated in his thoughts. The man wanted Tom to believe he could turn his life around.

But it was too late for Tom, wasn't it? He'd been a part of multiple robberies, witnessed his brothers shoot and kill a half a dozen times. Wasn't it too late for him to be redeemed?

Walt was certain he only deserved jail time. And Walt was the one who mattered.

The best thing, the easiest thing, was to move on. Surely when all of Ida's family were taking their leave, he could use the distraction to sneak away.

Someone had to have the key to his shackles. He just needed to know who. He was a decent pickpocket. He could slip it off them when they weren't paying attention. The homestead was more isolated than he would've liked—it was a fair piece to the next town and a railroad or stage—but the family had a barn full of horses.

For the first time in his life, he felt a pang of— was it conscience?—at the thought of stealing from Ida's family. He'd never really considered how stealing might affect the folks left behind.

With thoughts and plans and worries filling his mind, he drifted off to sleep again and was roused to a soft sound from the room next to his.

It was still dark outside. Only a bare hint of light graced the horizon out the window.

What had woken him?

The sound came again a few moments later. Louder this time. A woman crying out.

Was that Ida?

He had been so caught up in the family's Christmas celebrations that he hadn't done as much reconnaissance as he could've. He didn't know if Ida was in the room next to his or whether someone was sharing it with her.

Another soft cry came, and he closed his eyes, straining to hear better. Definitely Ida.

A second voice sounded. Good. That was good. She wasn't alone. Ida gave a soft gasp. The second voice murmured. And then, if he wasn't mistaken, he heard the sound of quiet sobs.

Had Ida woken up from a nightmare, like he had?

The thought made his stomach clench.

That first morning in the jailhouse, she'd had fine lines around her eyes. He'd thought at the time that she looked unrested.

Was she suffering from nightmares after what they'd gone through?

He'd been so self-centered, he hadn't thought enough about the scars she must bear after their ordeal.

He knew his brothers. Knew how to work around their tempers and keep their focus away from him. He'd seen gunshot wounds before.

One of their cousins had been a part of the gang for a few months when Tom had been seventeen. During a stagecoach robbery, he'd been shot and fatally wounded. Tom had been the one to carry his body to the hideout and later tasked with burying it.

He knew that every time he and his brothers left to commit a crime, they were riding into danger. It was the price they paid for the life they lived.

But Ida hadn't asked for any of that. She'd grown up in a loving, stable family.

He hadn't been kidding when he'd told her she was special. And for one moment while her eyes had been shining up at him, he'd almost asked her to escape with him.

Thankfully, his reason had returned.

He couldn't ask her to go on the run. He'd be living a life just like the one he'd left behind, always looking over his shoulder. Always living in the shadows.

She wouldn't want that. He didn't want that for her.

He was a fool for even thinking it.

She'd offered him her friendship, and he'd taken what she gave freely without a single thought.

He didn't want to hurt her.

And the deeper he let their friendship become, the more she would be hurt when he escaped.

It was... difficult for him to consider her feelings, her needs above his own.

Walt would come home later this morning. Tom would walk away without looking back, because it was the right thing to do.

For her.

CHAPTER 9

Something was different about Tom this morning.

A fine snow had begun to blow across the yard, but he made no mention of it nor joined in the children's conversation as they discussed it.

He was quieter than usual as Cecilia and John and the children took their leave just after breakfast. Ricky, Daisy, and Chester followed soon after.

She'd thought Tom would be shooting her secret smiles or otherwise teasing about the kiss they'd shared, but he seemed distracted. Subdued.

Breanna and Adam planned to leave just before lunch, but before Adam had brought all the luggage out to the wagon, Walt arrived on horseback.

He was alone. Apparently Libby's visit had gone

well and she'd decided to spend a few more days with her parents.

Ida shelled peas in the middle of the table. Walt and Pa settled at one end. Walt had Archie on his knee and nursed a cup of coffee. Tom sat on the sofa, his head bent over Edith's reading primer while she pointed at one of the pages.

"How are things?" Walt asked.

Ida still had a hard time reconciling this Walt with the brother she'd run into on that southbound train. Gone was his deep-seated anger, his sense of urgency to be on the job. He seemed more settled, somehow.

"Breanna surprised everyone when she showed up, and she's been keeping us all on our toes," Pa said.

Breanna called from the other room, obviously listening in as they chatted. "I know life is dull as dirt when I'm not here. Have you seen Archie's green mitten?"

Papa got up from the table to help her find it.

Walt turned to Ida. "And how has it been with Tom?"

Her brother's keen stare brought heat stinging to her cheeks, but she pretended not to feel it. "Why don't you ask Andrew? He's been keeping tabs on

Tom the entire time." But Andrew hadn't come in from putting Walt's horse in the barn.

Walt's stare turned considering. "I'm asking you."

Her gaze went to Tom, who still had his head bent near Edith's and didn't appear to be listening. "He is not like his brothers," she said in a low voice.

"In what way?"

"He told me he has never hurt an innocent."

To her surprise, Walt didn't ask whether she believed Tom. In fact, he said nothing.

"He seems almost... lonely," she added.

Tom presented a charming, confident front. But she didn't think the snatches of vulnerability that she'd seen over the past few days had been an act.

"Isn't there anything you can do?"

Walt held his silence. He looked serious but also contemplative. "Tom and his brothers have hurt a lot of people. They're responsible for robberies all over the West."

She knew that. She struggled with the fact that Tom hadn't walked away from his brothers. But she also saw something deeper in him.

Breanna and her husband came to the table, coats in hand.

Walt shifted in his seat. "Temperatures were falling as I rode out. Feels like a storm is coming in."

"The almanac called for heavy storms in the new few weeks," Adam said.

Breanna's lips twitched as if she were holding back a smile.

"Might be best to hunker down here. Leave in a few days, once the weather clears," Walt said.

"You know your mama would love to have you stay longer," Pa said.

"If it hits hard, train won't run," Walt added. "We'll see what the afternoon holds, but I might have to detain Tom here a little longer."

If the train wasn't running, that meant Ida could breathe easy for a few more days. She didn't have to make a decision about her future just yet.

Tom looked up from his place on the sofa.

Walt stood and reached for the coat he'd hung on the back of his chair. "Chores probably got set back with all the company here. I can help out in the barn."

"I'll help." Tom's offer made Walt's brows twitch, though he quickly blanked his expression.

Tom went on. "I've had these shackles on for days. I need to stretch my legs, even if you have to train your gun on me the whole time."

"You think you can muck stalls with that cast on?" Walt asked skeptically.

"I'll figure it out."

Walt shrugged. "It'll save me doing the work."

Breanna and her husband spoke in low tones as Walt went into the kitchen and returned with a small key that fit Tom's shackles.

"We'll stay tonight and see what the weather does," Breanna told Pa.

After Walt and Tom walked out, Breanna raised her brows. "Should we sneak over and watch? There's still a good-sized hole where you can see down from the hayloft."

Ida smiled.

"I have a feeling one of them is going to get into trouble," Breanna said.

Ida thought about the way Tom had barely looked at her this morning. Something was going on. She didn't know what. It was possible Tom was simply restless.

Or maybe he was planning something.

She and Breanna donned their coats and crossed the yard to the barn. Walt noticed when they snuck through the big double doors, which were open a crack. Tom's head and shoulders were visible in one of the stalls, but he didn't look their way as Ida followed Breanna up the wooden ladder and into the loft.

The hay smelled sweet, and even the way it scratched her bare skin was familiar. She hadn't been up here in years. Once upon a time, she'd loved to spy on her older brothers as they'd done chores.

Walt had been right to question whether Tom could work with his cast on. He was awkward as he maneuvered the pitchfork with his left hand and tried to balance it over his right arm.

But he was making it work. His face had gained some color and he was breathing hard, but he seemed fine.

It wasn't long before Andrew entered sideways through the door. Then Oscar and Edgar and Matty, who wouldn't want to be working outside in this blustery weather. Seb was the last to join.

While the brothers stood chatting and catching up with Walt, Seb manned the wheelbarrow, pushing it toward Tom, though he didn't speak to him.

The brothers were getting louder as Edgar teased Walt.

"Who do you think will throw the first punch?" Breanna whispered. It seemed their brothers could never get together without roughousing of some kind.

"Andrew." Ida had watched her brother for two days. If he were a pot of boiling water, his lid would be rattling. He'd been so tense and watchful over Tom's presence that he was spoiling for a fight.

They were both wrong. It was Ricky who slugged Edgar in the arm for some slight—real or imagined.

Edgar shouted, and Tom's head jerked up. He lost his hold on the pitchfork, which clattered to the ground. Tom bent to pick it up.

Seb said something that Ida couldn't hear and Tom nodded.

But when he stood back up, Tom's shoulders were tense as he watched Edgar and Ricky tussle in earnest. Edgar got in one punch to Ricky's kidney, but then Ricky managed to get his older brother in a headlock.

The way Tom reacted now reminded her of how he'd responded when an argument had broken out during the marbles tournament.

Was his reaction so quick because of the life he'd lived? She could only imagine that he'd had to hone his instincts to stay on Hector and Tristan's good side. And be on alert for any disagreement between the brothers, who probably didn't pull their punches.

What kind of life was that, forced to be on alert at every moment? To be wary of any noise or movement, watching for danger constantly?

"Adam thinks he has a story to tell," Breanna

whispered. She nodded to Tom when Ida sent her a questioning glance.

"He's been thinking of writing a book," Breanna went on. "If we stay, he may try to get Tom to open up. Share about his childhood. How he became... what he is today."

Would Tom want that? He was a private person, though he'd shared snippets of himself with her.

"Would you talk to him for Adam? See if he's open to it?" Breanna whispered.

As if he'd heard their whispered conversation, Tom looked up into the rafters. His gaze immediately rested on Ida. He didn't smile or wave, but tenderness filled his expression, if for only a breath of time.

"Please," Breanna whispered.

Ida'd started to care about Tom. Would it help or hurt him to talk about his childhood with Adam?

She didn't know.

But it couldn't hurt to ask.

———

If Tom had hoped the exertion of working in the barn would clear away the unsettled feeling he'd fought all day, he was disappointed.

He followed Walt toward the house, still without

his shackles. The snow was thicker now, and it seemed to blow in circles, riding on a wind that was cold enough to cut through a man down to his bones.

Tom felt physically tired, his muscles sore and his ribs issuing a constant hum of pain. The past two days of inactivity had done him well, but he wasn't healed yet.

But the hole inside him, the one that had opened up when Edith had given him an affectionate embrace, had expanded into a chasm.

Ida's brothers were rowdy and obnoxious, but it was clear they loved each other. Along with Jonas, they'd built the homestead to what it was today.

They took care of each other.

Walt waved goodbye to Oscar, Edgar, and Matty as they split off to their own homes on the ranch. When they were gone, the lawman watched the slate-gray sky as if he were looking for some kind of answer there.

Tom didn't care about the snow except that it made him itchy. He never stayed in one place long. The risk of being caught was too high.

He and Walt kicked snow off their boots at the porch steps. The house would seem emptier without so much company. Maybe that was a good thing. He needed his wits about him if he was going to come up with an escape plan. And to keep his distance from Ida.

He'd determined to stay away after hearing her wake up in tears. He refused to contribute to any more of her nightmares.

It would've been better if Walt had insisted on taking him back to the jail cell in town right away.

Maybe the marshal was slipping. He'd forgotten to put Tom's shackles back on as they traipsed inside. Tom enjoyed every normal stride he took.

The shackles stayed off but the snow stuck as the afternoon wore on.

Tom wouldn't be able to hike through blizzard conditions. Which meant he was stuck, too.

The noon meal of soup and thick buttered bread was served. With only Breanna's family, Jonas and Penny, and Walt and Andrew in the house, it felt positively bare.

He steeled himself as she sat down for the meal at his elbow. She and her sister had been cooking up some plan up in the rafters. He'd seen the mischievous smiles they'd shared.

"Adam wants to interview you for a project he's working on," she whispered as the food was passed after the prayer.

He sent her a skeptical look. "I'm not going to incriminate myself."

Her lips twitched as she tried to stave off a smile. It didn't work, and when she smiled, he felt it to his bones.

Her eyes danced. "Not that kind of interview. I think he's more interested in learning about your childhood. Your background."

Tom sipped the soup, pretending to think about it. He didn't want to share that with anyone.

He was distracted by the taste of Penny's cooking. This was the best tasting soup he'd ever eaten.

Ida nudged his boot with hers.

As if he could forget she was there.

"You don't have to, if you don't want to," she whispered. She slipped the piece of bread from her plate to his, probably because she'd noticed his had already been devoured.

She was taking care of him.

It was too much.

"I'll do it," he muttered. He could make something up, if it came to that. "Provided we do it somewhere private."

Somewhere that he'd be away from Ida.

After lunch, Walt agreed to accompany the two men to the now-empty bunkhouse.

Tom sat in a hardback chair, Adam nearby with a pencil and sheaf of papers at hand. He pulled a small table in front of himself. Walt lay down in one of the bunks and tipped his hat over his face, as if he would go to sleep.

It was awkward just sitting there, staring at the other man.

"Aren't you going to ask me some questions?"

Adam smiled. "We can do it that way if you like." He tapped his pencil on the small table. "What's your earliest memory?"

Tom shook his head. Adam didn't want to hear about that.

He'd been ill, feverish and maybe even a little delirious, and he'd gotten up from his bed to ask one of his older brothers for some water. They'd been talking in low voices over a table—a kitchen table? Tom couldn't even remember the house or shack where they'd been staying.

He'd gotten smacked for interrupting.

He cleared his throat. "I remember snitchin' some cans of tinned ham from a mercantile when I was real small," he said instead.

Adam was a journalist. He wanted something sensational, right?

"How old were you?"

Tom shrugged. "Five? Six?"

"Did someone tell you to do it? One of your brothers?"

Tom sat back in the chair, stretching his legs out

in front of him, enjoying the ability to do so since he was still unhampered by the leg irons. "I don't remember."

Now that he'd opened up his memory bank, he could feel again the gnawing hunger that felt like his guts were trying to eat his body from the inside out.

He couldn't remember why he'd been so hungry.

Maybe his brothers had left him behind while they'd gone out. They hadn't started using him as a lookout until he was almost ten.

He had a lot of memories of being alone and bored, tossing a ball against the wall and catching it. Drawing on whatever scraps of paper he could find with a tiny nub of a pencil.

He shook those thoughts away. This fellow didn't want to hear about that, either.

"I was hungry, so I took something that wasn't mine."

Walt never moved a muscle.

Tom considered heading back to the house. This trip down memory lane wasn't comfortable. He didn't like remembering how lonely he'd been. Or how many times he'd wished for a friend. Or how he'd wished that his brothers would play with him or even say something kind to him instead of barking orders.

He'd always been afraid of them and their tempers.

He must've been all of seven when he had seen Tristan stab another man, who may or may not have been cheating at cards.

Tristan had caught sight of Tom huddled in the corner. He was supposed to be asleep. Tristan had grabbed Tom's collar and shaken him, threatening that if he ever told what he'd seen, he'd get the same treatment.

Tom had never told.

And he wasn't going to now.

But the thought of walking back into the house where Ida would look at him with soft eyes... Where he couldn't help but want. Want her, want to be in her presence, to be in her life.

He couldn't go back in there.

So he sat where he was and kept talking.

CHAPTER 10

"Would you mind very much... giving me a shave?"

Tom asked Ida's father the question and saw the brief flash of surprise in the older man's eyes.

Tom had made it a point not to ask for anything during his time on the Whites' homestead, but he had little choice.

After snowing ferociously for five days, the blizzard had blown itself out before dawn that morning. Walt planned to get Tom to town early tomorrow.

Tonight was his last night on the homestead. His last chance to take a walk with Ida.

And he didn't intend to do it with ten days' worth of stubble on his chin.

Jonas nodded. "I'll grab my razor and meet you in your bedroom."

Tom walked there without the clink of chains accompanying him. He didn't kid himself that Walt trusted him. Anybody who took off on foot during a blizzard like they'd just experienced deserved to freeze to death.

Tom wasn't that stupid.

He dragged a straight-backed chair to the center of the room and sat as Jonas toted in a bowl of steaming water. He had a white towel thrown over his arm, and Tom could see the flash of silver that must be the razor peeking from his hip pocket.

Jonas worked up a lather with some shaving soap and spread it across Tom's jaw and neck while Tom stared at the ceiling.

"Don't move," he warned.

Did he think Tom had asked him in here to have a chat? He was all talked out after the past days. He'd spent hours upon hours in the bunkhouse with Adam, telling far too many stories about his life. The man knew how to coax information by the questions he asked.

After holding everything inside for such a long time, it was almost a relief for Tom to talk about growing up with his brothers. Some of the crimes he'd seen them commit.

He'd steered clear of talking about any involvement he'd had with robberies and holdups.

But he'd thought about them plenty. After spending so much time with Ida's family, he felt... regretful about the things he'd done.

When he hadn't been in the bunkhouse with Adam, he'd gone to the barn. Seb had made a comment that the barn had never been so clean, nor the horses so well-groomed.

Tom had done everything he could to steer clear of Ida.

"You and my daughter have gotten pretty close," Jonas said now.

Tom had to wait for the man to lift away the razor before he swallowed. Hard. "I care about her."

No matter what he'd done, he hadn't been able to escape her. He'd stopped trying.

After dinner, they'd spent hours by the fire, playing dominoes or checkers. He knew her doctor brother had a traveling nurse job lined up for her in Sweetwater County. He'd seen her hesitation about taking it and knew what that must stem from. She was afraid, and that was his fault.

She would be good as a nurse. She was a natural caregiver.

His feelings for her had opened inside him like a

terrifying abyss. He didn't want his time with her to end.

But Walt wasn't going to change his mind, even though he'd listened to most of Tom's conversations with Adam. He'd even asked for clarification a couple of times.

Walt still counted him a criminal, though he seemed to have lost the anger and bitterness that he'd expressed during those first hours together on the train.

Jonas swiped the razor up Tom's neck and beneath his chin again, the blade scraping his skin with its distinctive sound. It seemed as if he took an extra moment to wipe away the shaving soap on the cloth he'd thrown over his arm. "And after you're gone?"

What would happen to Ida after Tom was gone? Was that what her father meant?

Tom blinked, using the fraction of a second to try and swallow the emotion that rose up in him.

"She's going to Sweetwater County," Tom said. "I'm sure she'll forget about me soon enough." Despite her fear, she'd end up going. She was too strong to let the fear win.

Single men would notice someone as pretty and vivacious as Ida. She would meet someone—

someone with a normal upbringing, someone on the right side of the law—and fall in love.

"So you don't intend to write to her?"

There were several more scratches of the razor before Tom could form words.

From prison. He heard the words Jonas hadn't said.

"No." He wouldn't pretend, not now.

He wasn't going to end up at that penitentiary.

And that meant he couldn't write to Ida. Not when he was on the run, a wanted criminal.

Besides, she deserved better than him.

There was silence as Jonas continued, the razor now at the left side of Tom's jaw.

Jonas didn't have to speak to fill the silence. He often received teasing from his family for his quiet ways, always listening more than he spoke. From what Tom had seen over the past few days, his reputation was well-deserved.

Jonas had earned respect as the head of his household, and he didn't have to manhandle anyone or shout to have it.

For a moment, all of the feelings that had overcome Tom during the past few days as he'd recounted his story to Adam welled up.

He wished he'd known someone like Jonas

during his tumultuous childhood. What if he had met someone who'd taught him good from evil?

No, Tom knew. He'd known that the crimes he'd helped his brothers commit were wrong, and he'd participated anyway.

At first, he'd felt as if he didn't have a choice. And then, after a while, he'd become numb to the voice inside that told him it was wrong to steal. He'd had to ignore it, or he'd have gone crazy.

But what if he'd had someone to guide him? Someone to step in and give him the opportunity to make a different decision?

There was no changing the past now.

Tom was still practicing being perfectly still. Jonas was in his line of sight when the man nodded to the book lying on the end of Tom's bed.

His face flushed. Until now, he didn't think anyone had noticed that the Bible he'd nicked from the living room was missing.

"You been reading that?" Jonas asked.

He didn't sound angry.

"A little."

That was it. No berating Tom for taking it without permission. No demanding to know whether Tom believed what the book said.

Tom was left to muddle through his own thoughts.

He heard himself ask the question. "Seb said something to me a few days ago."

Jonas waited for Tom to go on.

"He said he believes any man can be redeemed."

Tom had blown Seb off with a quick retort. But he hadn't been able to forget the words.

Jonas nodded.

Tom had to wait while the older man shaved the small space between his mouth and nose before he could speak again. "Do you believe that too?"

Jonas passed him a second towel, and Tom used it to wipe off his face, slumping forward in the seat so his elbows rested on his knees.

Jonas waited until he looked up before he spoke. "There's been plenty of times I needed redeeming."

What? Really?

What did a family man like Jonas need to be redeemed from?

"Sometimes a man has to ask for help," Jonas said.

Seb had said something similar. But Tom had never had anyone to ask before. It wasn't his right to ask Jonas for help, or even Walt. He didn't belong to this family. And he never would.

He passed one hand over his eyes.

The best he could hope for was a sweet goodbye from Ida.

Nothing more.

———

"WOULD you go for a walk with me?"

Ida looked up from the knitting in her lap—she'd been forced to start over on a baby blanket for Breanna since the other had been lost—to find Tom standing in front of her with her coat and scarf in one hand.

He'd shaved, and the sight of his handsome face without the whiskers sent a jolt of attraction through her.

He wore the red scarf around his neck, his expression unreadable.

She glanced at his feet, though she hadn't seen him wear the leg irons since the blizzard had blown in.

Her gaze jumped to Walt, sitting at the table with a half-eaten piece of pie they'd enjoyed at lunch. He had a pencil in hand. Probably writing to Libby.

Tom followed her gaze and must've guessed at her concern. His expression didn't change as he asked, "You mind if I take your sister for a walk? Say goodbye?"

Goodbye. Ida's breath caught in her chest. She wasn't ready.

Walt nodded. "Stay in sight of the house."

In the kitchen, Tom helped her slip into her coat, the brush of his fingers warm against her shoulders through the fabric of her dress.

She'd missed his touch. He'd spent far more time with Adam and Walt and Seb the last few days than with her.

Last night when she had excused herself to go to bed, the four men had been sitting at the kitchen table, talking in low voices.

She was glad for Tom's sake. She knew how much he wanted to belong. She wanted it for him.

But she missed their closeness.

She'd missed him so deeply that yesterday morning she had snuck out and huddled in her coat beneath the bunkhouse window, listening while Tom and Adam had talked. The window was drafty, allowing her to hear everything Tom had said about watching his brothers beat up a stagecoach driver and leave him for dead.

Tom had been thirteen.

Her heart had broken for the boy he'd been. He'd lived with fear and violence his whole life.

He'd spoken of his brothers' actions almost dispassionately, as if he was separate from them.

But how did a boy witness something like that without it becoming a part of him?

Tom had suffered at his brothers' hands, when it should've been their job to protect and care for him.

She hated the other Seymours.

But she also refused to let them steal this moment—or the rest of her life—from her. She was determined to tell Maxwell she'd take the job in Sweetwater County. The restful days at home had been what she needed. She wasn't whole, not yet, but she was getting there.

She just had to get through the next few hours.

She'd overheard Walt say that he and Tom would leave at daybreak tomorrow. After that, she would never see Tom again.

She wasn't ready for this goodbye, but she pulled her mittens out of her coat pocket and followed Tom out the door anyway.

It was still early, but there had only been a few days since the winter solstice, and the days were short. It would only be a matter of minutes before twilight came.

Walt followed them onto the porch, and for a moment Ida wondered if he was going to walk along with them.

But he stayed where he was, and she and Tom strolled without speaking past the barn and then farther.

There was a brisk wind that had her tucking her chin into the folds of her scarf.

"I suppose Walt can see you at a fair distance with that scarf on," she teased. It was the best she could do since her throat already felt hot and tight with tears.

Tom reached out and threaded her arm through the crook of his elbow. "He knows he doesn't need to worry. I wouldn't miss this time with you."

It was a sweet thing to say.

"Mama and I put together a basket for you to take on the train. I made some apple cake."

He smiled and squeezed her arm. "I thought I smelled cinnamon coming from the kitchen earlier. I hope you don't expect me to share with your brother."

He sounded completely unaffected while she was breaking apart. She took a deep breath to try and steady herself, but it didn't help.

"And you'll be leaving for your new job soon."

"How did you know I'd decided?"

He shrugged. "Are you finished packing?"

She elbowed him in the side for the tease. So what if she liked to be organized and have things planned ahead?

Tomorrow, she would be excited about her new job and the possibilities that stretched in front of her. Excited to meet new families and share her skills with those that needed them. Tonight, she could only feel her heart breaking.

They passed several more strides in silence.

"Aren't you going to ask me to write to you?" Tom asked finally. "Or if I'll ever come back?"

He stopped walking. She glanced behind her and could see Walt on the porch and one of her brothers working with a horse in the corral.

She turned back to face Tom, who took her mittened hands in his larger ones.

"Of course not," she scoffed. She wouldn't wish for the impossible. She tried to hike up her chin, but it wobbled.

His eyes flicked that direction—or was it to her mouth? Either way, he had to have seen her emotion.

She drew in a stinging breath through her nose and tried to blink the tears away.

He breathed her name, drawing her close. His arms wrapped around her, and he tucked her head beneath his chin.

"I never wanted my life to be any different. Not until now." He breathed the words into her hair.

Her arms slid around his waist, and she breathed in his scent—horses and hay from working out in the barn, a hint of her father's shaving soap, and the aroma of the man himself.

She tipped her head back so she could see him. "Aren't you going to kiss me goodbye?"

He shifted so that his face was pressed into the place where her shoulder met her neck, his breath hot on her skin through her scarf. He groaned, his hands gripping tighter at her waist.

"No. No matter how much I want to, the answer is no."

What kind of answer was that? He wanted to kiss her goodbye, but he wasn't going to? Even though this was the last time they would be together?

"Why not?" She knew he must be able to hear the tears that were so close to the surface.

His voice, when he answered, was muffled through her scarf. "I'm trying to do the right thing."

Since when? She put her hands on his shoulders and pushed, and he straightened, though neither one stepped away. Now they were face-to-face.

"So am I," she whispered. And then she raised up on tiptoe and lifted her chin and kissed him.

Maybe he was trying to do the right thing—however he had decided what that was—but his resolve didn't last past the first brush of her lips against his. His hands left her waist and curved behind her back, pulling her a half step closer until there was no distance between them. His kiss was tender and sad and hopeful and sorrowful. And it tasted of finality.

He was the one who broke the embrace. He took a step back and half-turned away. He rubbed the back of his neck and exhaled a shuddering sigh.

"I've never met anyone like you," he said. For one second, he turned his face toward her, and she saw the maelstrom of emotions she'd thought absent only moments before. He was burning up from the inside out.

And then he blinked, and his expression smoothed.

He reached forward to brush a strand of hair behind her ear, his touch tender.

And then he tucked her arm in his again and turned them back toward the house.

There was no attempt at escape. No attempt at talking her into helping him.

He didn't ask her to ride to town with him in the morning. Maybe that was pride, him not wanting her to see him behind bars again.

Whatever the case, when they neared the porch, he brushed a kiss on her cheek and whispered, "Goodbye."

CHAPTER 11

"Tom?"

Ida hated the way her voice wavered. She mustered what courage she could to demand, "What are you doing?"

It was too dark in the barn to see much, but she knew it was him by the way he moved. How could that be possible after they'd spent such a short time together?

He had gone still at her words, but she knew he was in the first stall. Oscar's big bay horse was kept there.

"Go back to the house."

His voice sounded strange, disjointed in the darkness.

She didn't leave. "What are you doing out here?"

She hadn't been asleep, though the hour was late.

She couldn't stop thinking about Tom and his goodbye kiss.

Some instinct or uncomfortable feeling had pushed her to sit up in bed, her quilt wrapped around her. In the bright moonlight, she had seen his long strides eating up the space between the house and the barn.

Unshackled.

Why had Walt left him without the leg irons?

She hadn't taken the time to dress. She'd thrown her coat on over her nightgown and shoved her feet into boots and gone after him.

"I thought you were different." Her voice was trembling again, and she swallowed hard.

"You thought wrong." His voice sounded hard and distant.

Metal tinked against metal. He'd been in the barn for maybe a minute while she had fumbled into her coat and boots. Did he have a saddle in there?

Why hadn't she woken anyone else? Her conscience screamed at her.

She moved to stand in the stall door, blocking his way out.

"If you do this…" *It will break my heart.* "Walt will come after you. He'll never stop chasing you."

Tom had a saddle on the huge horse.

His arm jerked as he finished cinching it.

When he turned, he seemed so much bigger than her in the darkness that for a moment fear won. She flinched away from him.

He caught her against him, his voice was rough and urgent. "Whatever I said was just to get you to trust me. Walt, too. So I could get rid of those shackles. That's it."

His words battered her. *No.*

And he wasn't done yet. "Do you really think someone like you could tempt me? Make me want to change my ways?" He laughed, the sound harsh and low.

She was frozen, hurt. Her heart was shattered at her feet.

Her thoughts spun like they'd been tossed in a swirling windstorm.

Should she scream? Or run? The barn was an equal distance to both Oscar's place and the big house. Surely someone would hear her.

Her brothers had been watching so closely for all these days. Someone would come.

She was shaking, undecided. She'd thought…

She registered the feel of his hands at her waist. His words were hard, but his hands remained gentle.

For a moment, he went perfectly still, even holding his breath. What was he listening for?

What was going on?

And then he bundled her toward the horse, shoving her when she didn't move fast enough.

"Tom, what—?"

"Shut up," he whispered.

He tossed her onto the saddle, and she would've gone all the way over to escape from the other side, but the bay was so tall that she worried she'd break her arm if she landed badly when she hit the ground.

She clung to the saddle horn instead. She had barely righted herself when he gained the saddle behind her. She heard his soft grunt and knew the movement must've jostled his ribs.

The horse danced beneath them, and Ida struggled as Tom's casted arm banded around her waist. His jaw pressed into her skull behind her ear. "Stop."

There was a scrape of something sharp against wood. The sound of a match striking, she thought.

Light flared and illuminated a face she had hoped she would never see again.

Hector.

"Just what do you think you're trying to pull, boy?"

Tom's brothers stood just inside the barn doors.

———

TOM FELT IDA'S TREMOR.

She'd stopped struggling the moment his brothers had revealed themselves.

Hector held a candle stub aloft, and the flickering light cast shadows on their faces.

"Not trying anything," Tom said. "I'm getting out of here."

If his brothers had planned for a long confrontation, they didn't get it. Tom nudged the horse with his heels, and the animal bolted forward.

He had the element of surprise, and his brothers were forced to jump out of the way or be trampled. He used his foot in the stirrup to kick Tristan as they rushed past.

His mind was racing as the horse galloped across the yard, away from the house. From the corner of his eye, he caught sight of the two horses in the shadows around the side of the barn. His brothers must have ridden in.

This wasn't good. None of this had been part of the plan.

Ida was supposed to be asleep in her bed, not coming out to the barn and pleading with him to make a better choice.

His brothers were supposed to find him farther from the house.

It didn't matter what had gone wrong. Tom had

to get Ida as far away from the danger as he could.

He'd known they would come. Known it would be tonight.

The blizzard had delayed Walt too long. His brothers had had too much time to figure out where Tom was hiding.

Hiding. That was it.

He could hear hoofbeats behind him, gaining ground.

His brothers would shoot if they had to, and with the moon full and bright like it was, he and Ida on horseback made much too clear of a target.

He'd struck a plan with Walt and was supposed to lead his brothers straight to the little valley behind Edgar's place, but he couldn't do it. Not with Ida in harm's way. Back at the barn, he'd heard someone approaching and his instinct had said it was his brothers.

He'd known he had to get her out of there.

And now he couldn't take the chance she'd get shot. The images of his nightmare from days ago played behind his eyes.

Edgar had warned him on that first morning that the brothers knew every nook and cranny on the land.

If the White boys knew every hiding place, Ida would too. She'd grown up there and followed her brothers around as a child. She'd played in every gully and had swum in the creek.

He turned his horse into the woods, forced to slow the animal so they wouldn't crash into a tree.

"We need a hiding place, fast."

She was silent. Seeing his brothers again must've filled her with terror. She hadn't made a sound since Hector lit that candle.

He tightened his arm around her waist. "I won't let them get to you. I promise. Where can we hide? Someplace that's big enough for both of us."

"There's a fallen log." Her voice shook, but she didn't let that stop her. "Up the creek, about a hundred yards. The water washed out a place beneath it, sort of a depression underneath."

He pressed the reins into her hands, trusting her to get them there.

She urged the horse forward, weaving around the trees on instinct.

He could hear his brothers' horses crashing through the underbrush behind them.

Ida reined in.

He threw his leg over and slid off the horse, landing with a thud that jarred his ribs. He bit back a word she wouldn't appreciate and reached up to pull her off the horse. He slapped the animal's rump, and the horse took off. Tom didn't know whether the horse galloping away would be enough of a distraction, but he had to try.

Ida grabbed his hand and tugged him to the creekbank, where a large log had indeed fallen and created a pool off to the side of the creek. She was quick to throw her leg over it and then her foot splashed into shallow water on the other side.

He followed, wincing when he twisted wrong and the pain in his side barked. He urged her to crawl, keeping the log between them and his brothers.

She was right. Years of the creek lapping at the muddy bank had created a washed-out hole underneath the log. Someone had been down here recently, breaking the ice for the cattle that grazed the pasture just past the woods.

To hide there meant they had to lie in about an inch of water.

She did so without complaint, though she started shivering.

He put his arm around her, holding her and warming her as best he could.

She didn't struggle against him, but neither did she turn to him.

The moon shined from behind the log, throwing shadows that would hide them as long as he and Ida were still.

"It's all right," he whispered. "Your brothers will come."

She shook her head, her temple brushing his cheek. She didn't think they would come? Or she didn't want them to? He could understand if she was afraid for her family.

She turned her head so her mouth was near his ear. "I saw Hector drop the candle in the hay. The barn could go up in flames."

It was Tom's turn to shake his head. Every one of her brothers was out tonight. Jonas, too. They'd almost had to hogtie Andrew to get him to keep guard over the house. With all of them watching, someone would see if there was a blaze in the barn.

But she didn't know that.

And a fire could spread fast in a barn with hay in every stall.

He couldn't do anything about that now. He had to keep Ida safe.

Something big splashed downstream. Sounds of movement, like someone was guiding a horse through the water. Toward Tom and Ida's hiding place.

He wished he could turn his head and look, but he didn't dare move. He squeezed Ida as tightly as he dared, urging her to be still and silent.

The sounds grew closer, still moving through the water toward them.

He and Ida were still hidden. A walking horse wouldn't be able to jump the log. There was no reason for someone hunting them to come into the shallows here, not when the creek twisted away to the north.

They were safe. They had to be.

"Where are you, you lily-livered coward?" Tristan's growl was quiet, almost as if he were talking to himself. "I should've known you would turn traitor. Your mama was yellow-bellied, and I always knew you were too."

Tom flinched at the insult to his mother. He couldn't help it, but he hoped the slight movement was hidden in the shadows.

He held his breath, waiting for his brother to pass.

And then there was another sound. Hoofbeats, from multiple horses. He heard the sound of a hammer being drawn back, a gun cocked.

"Tristan, you're surrounded." Walt's voice carried clearly through the woods.

Beside him, Ida's quiet gasp was nearly inaudible.

"Throw your gun on the ground," Walt continued. "My deputy's a sharpshooter. And my brother can hit a squirrel at thirty yards. You're not getting away this time."

Tom heard the way the water splashed and knew his brother must've kicked his mount.

A shot rang out, and Tristan howled.

Ida jumped, and Tom pressed his jaw to her cheek, praying she wouldn't cry out.

Tristan was still too close. If he found them, he would shoot—

Another horse closed in. And a second one.

"Watch out. I only winged him," came a voice Tom couldn't place.

There was a sound of scuffling, more splashing of water, and then Walt's voice, clear as day. "I've got him. Knocked his weapon loose. Somebody bring me some rope."

Ida took a hitching breath which Tom realized was a soft sob.

"We got them both." Walt's voice rang out in the darkness, calm and unruffled. "We need to find Tom."

Relief flooded through Tom, and he exhaled a breath he hadn't realized he was still holding.

"It's all right," he murmured to Ida, then pushed out of the hole. "We're over here," he called. "Unarmed." Just in case the marshal or someone in his posse got any ideas.

"We?" That voice had to belong to Oscar, and it was close, too, several yards behind their hiding place.

"I've got Ida with me."

He got to his feet and reached down to help Ida to hers.

Once she was standing and away from the shadows of the fallen tree, the moonlight washed her face white. She was muddy, bedraggled, her hair loose around her shoulders. And she was crying.

There were more voices in the darkness. Tom didn't hear what they said because he couldn't look away from Ida, though she wouldn't look at him.

And then Oscar and Seb were there, moving between the two of them. Seb picked her up and carried her away from the hiding place.

It was chaos for a few minutes. Walt had amassed a bigger posse than Tom knew about. Maybe he was smarter than Tom had given him credit for.

Tom was hustled toward the bunkhouse, past the still-standing barn. No flames licked from the structure and Tom exhaled his relief.

He was unceremoniously shoved inside the bunkhouse, which was filled with too many lamps, too bright after their time in the darkness.

Ida was there. She was alone.

Someone had thrown a blanket around her shoulders, and she sat shivering on one of the bunks.

He was shivering, too, more from the terror of what could've happened to her than the feel of his clammy clothes against his chilled skin. If his brothers had shown up sixty seconds earlier, he wouldn't have had the horse saddled. If he hadn't been able to get Ida out of there...

But he didn't go to her like he wanted.

The door opened, and Walt entered, shutting it behind himself firmly.

"The barn—?" Ida asked, her teeth chattering.

"Andrew saw Hector and Tristan out there. Once they were gone, he came out to stomp out the flames. Everything's fine."

Tears flooded Ida's eyes, and she pressed the blanket over her face. And then, she straightened. So strong and brave.

Walt focused on Tom. "Matty and my two best deputies are taking your brothers straight to the jail cells in town. They're trussed up good, but I'm going to join them just to make sure they don't try anything. We'll be heading out on the early train tomorrow."

Tom nodded, his eyes shifting to Ida. She stared

at Walt as if she couldn't comprehend his words at all.

Tom was worried about her. Had someone checked her over? She was pale and silent.

He wanted to go to her, hold her. Comfort her.

But the way she was looking at him, her brows drawn with dawning comprehension, he knew he couldn't.

"She needs to get to the house," Walt muttered to Tom. "Before she gets hypothermia."

Ida's chin kicked up, and Tom knew her brother had played to her natural independence.

Walt went on. "As far as I'm concerned, there was some chaos out in the woods and you disappeared while we were capturing your brothers."

Walt held a steady gaze on Tom.

It was the deal they'd struck, the one Walt had offered when Tom had gone to him the day before. He'd known his brothers were coming, known that tonight would be the night, with the snow no longer falling and the moon full.

Until that moment, he hadn't been sure the marshal would hold to his end of the bargain.

Ida looked between the two men with wide eyes. "You planned this?" she whispered.

Walt nodded.

Tom just held her stare.

"You weren't supposed to get involved," Tom said apologetically. "I was supposed to be further from the house when they caught up to me."

"And then he was going to lead them straight into my posse," Walt said.

She nodded, tears standing in her eyes.

I'm sorry. The words stuck in his throat. She was everything to him, and he had scared her good tonight. *Sorry for all of it.*

He couldn't stay. He knew that. He was still a wanted man. Walt had offered him his freedom, but he knew the offer was short-lived. If any one of the deputies in town saw him, they'd arrest him and send him right to the judge, along with his brothers.

"I have to go," he said.

She nodded, blinking and turning her face to the side.

"Wait five minutes," Walt cautioned. "We should be cleared out by then."

Five minutes. Maybe he could try to right things with Ida—

But she stood up and went to her brother. "Can you walk me up to the house?"

Walt put his arm around her.

It nearly killed him, but Tom said nothing as they walked out of the bunkhouse.

CHAPTER 12

"Shut the door," Tom muttered.

He saw the marshal reach for his gun and stepped out from behind the tall bureau. He held both hands up to show that he was unarmed.

Walt raised one eyebrow so high that it almost hit the brim of his hat. He shut the door like Tom had asked.

It hadn't taken Tom much to track down Walt's room at the hotel in downtown Colorado Springs. He'd been a day behind Walt and the two deputies he'd taken with him to escort Tom's brothers.

Tom was still a wanted man and didn't want to show his face, so he'd snuck inside the hotel room and waited. He'd spent the day watching life happening on the street below.

"You need a shave," the marshal observed.

Tom shook his head. He didn't need the man's smart remarks. He needed answers. "Why did you help me?"

Walt had been after him and his brothers for years, according to the man himself and from everything his family had said.

"Was it because of your sister?"

"I wouldn't be a very good lawman if I let other people's emotions dictate what I do."

Tom had suspected that.

Which was why Walt letting Tom go didn't make sense.

"Why, then?"

Walt nodded to the pitcher of water on a table across the room. "You mind if I...?" He didn't wait for Tom to answer. He even turned his back to Tom as he splashed water on his face and washed his hands and then dried off with a towel from the same table.

That showed trust. The marshal would never have turned his back to Tom before they'd gotten on that train.

"You've made some bad choices," Walt said finally, turning to face him. "But I don't think you're all bad."

Did that mean the marshal believed him about his involvement in his brothers' crimes? That he'd only been indirectly involved? Never hurt anybody?

Walt held Tom's gaze, and some meaning filled his eyes. "Don't prove me wrong."

Walt seemed to think that was the end of it, but Tom wasn't done.

"If I take this deal you gave me," Tom started. He took a breath, blew it out. "If I run away, then I can't ever go back to Bear Creek."

Walt sat on the bed and began taking off his boots.

Tom hadn't asked a question. He already knew the answer.

He slipped his hand inside his coat and touched Ida's scarf. He'd stashed it in an inside pocket because the bright color made him too conspicuous. People would remember a man wearing a scarf that color. But he couldn't leave it behind. He wanted a piece of her with him, no matter how small.

"If I went with you, in front of that judge..." Tom took a deep breath. Was he really saying this? "If I testified against my brothers, do you think I would get a lighter sentence?"

He didn't know if that was something a judge would take into account. He didn't know if he could go through with it, turn on his brothers like that. *I always knew you were a lily-livered coward.*

He wasn't a boy anymore, though. He wasn't trapped with his brothers with nowhere else to go. For the first time in his life, he was free. Free to make his own decisions.

Even this one.

Walt tipped his head to the side, his eyes far-off as if he were considering Tom's question. "I don't know," he said finally. "There's a lot of people want to see the Seymour gang hang." And Tom was a Seymour.

"But it might work?"

Because at that moment, no matter how far he ran, Tom might be free in a sense. But not completely. If he was still wanted, he would be hiding for the rest of his life. Maybe if he went far enough away, made up a good enough story, he could have a semblance of a normal life. But his crimes would always be hanging over his head.

"I don't know," Walt said again. "Are you willing to risk it?"

————

IDA HADN'T SEEN Tom in almost seven months, not since she'd left the bunkhouse after that terrible night when Hector and Tristan had shown up on the family homestead.

It had taken her all of ten minutes to regret how she had walked out of the bunkhouse. She'd run inside and gotten dressed in dry clothes. But by the time she'd rushed back to the bunkhouse, she'd found it empty and dark.

Her father hugged her when she returned to the kitchen. He didn't say anything. He didn't have to.

She'd left for Sweetwater County two days later, and she'd kept herself busy with work ever since. All these months later, she'd made a route around six small towns in the county and had traveled among them numerous times. She'd made a difference.

In that time, she'd thought that her grief over losing Tom was waning, but he was the first thing she thought about when she stepped into the house after being away for so long.

The savory scent of Mama's beef stew, one of her favorites, surrounded her the moment she crossed the kitchen threshold. She was enveloped in a brief hug from Andrew before her mother got a hold of her.

"Walt and Libby surprised us not an hour ago. They're visiting for a few days."

That was welcome news. Ida and Libby had exchanged letters, though not as often as she would've liked.

Her brother had married Libby only a month

after that fateful train ride. His work still took him different places, but oftentimes Libby was able to go with him and do her nursing in whatever town or city she found herself in.

Between the two of them changing addresses so frequently, it was difficult to correspond.

Ida couldn't wait to see her friend.

She hesitated in the doorway when she saw Walt and Papa sitting at the table nursing cups of coffee. Their backs were turned, and neither one noticed her.

"I didn't think he could do it." Walt shook his head. "I thought for sure he would take the easy way out and go back to the life he had before. But he's proved me wrong."

"Does she know?"

Walt shrugged. "Dunno. He didn't ask about her, and I held off bringing her up, wondering if he would."

"Do you think he'll ever come back here?" Papa asked.

Ida's heart was beating in her throat. "Who are you talking about?"

Both men turned in surprise. Papa stood out of his chair, rushing to embrace her.

Walt wore an expression halfway between

chagrin and guilt as he took his turn to give her a hug.

She wasn't giving up that easily. "Who are you talking about? Who might come back?"

It couldn't be—

The men exchanged a look. Papa gave a small nod.

"Tom," Walt said almost reluctantly.

She was shocked into silence. She had hoped, but it had felt like a wild sort of hope, nearly impossible.

"I thought he disappeared. You let him go." If her voice held a slight note of accusation, she couldn't help it.

Walt shook his head. "He came back. Met up with me in Colorado. Went before the judge and testified against his brothers. I got Adam to wire me a copy of all the things Tom told him for his book. The judge pardoned him."

All of a sudden, her heart was thudding in her ears. Tom had been pardoned?

"Why didn't he—?" Why hadn't he written her? Come for her? "Why didn't you tell me?" she demanded instead.

Now Walt for sure looked guilty.

"Tom asked him not to." Libby was hurrying down the hallway. She embraced Ida, and the two stayed with arms linked around each other's waist as Ida turned back to her brother, waiting for his explanation.

"He was trying to make a fresh start," Walt said. "He started working for Daniel. Running papers around town. Doing odd jobs." Daniel was Fran and Emma's brother, who lived in Colorado and worked as an attorney.

"He's been working with Walt too," Libby offered.

Walt sighed and gave his wife a frustrated look before facing Ida to explain. "A couple of times I asked him to consult when I was hunting down some criminals. Tom had some different ideas of where they might be or what I should look for. He helped me catch two of them."

Tom was... helping the law? Would wonders never cease?

She didn't know what to think. Her mind was spinning. But the one thought that stuck was that, if Tom had wanted her to know he'd started over, he would have told her.

That thought solidified in her stomach, and it twisted.

"I'm happy for him." And she was even happier that her voice didn't tremble on the words. She smiled wanly. "I'm a little tired from the train ride." She pressed the back of her hand to her forehead. "I might lie down for just a few moments before supper."

She excused herself and went to her old bedroom. She quickly shut the door behind her and leaned against it, her eyes unseeing.

After everything, he hadn't wanted her. He'd gone on with his life. Stayed in Colorado.

She could be happy for him. She'd known how trapped he felt, with a potential prison sentence ahead of him and his brothers behind him. Now he was free.

She *would* be happy for him. Tomorrow.

She pressed her palm against her mouth and stifled a sob.

A knock on the door behind her rattled her.

She took two panting breaths. "I'm fine. I'll be out in a little while."

It was Libby's voice that carried through the door. "There's one more thing you should know. When we saw Tom two days ago, he was still wearing your scarf."

———

WAIT ON THE LORD.

Tom had read the words from the Good Book that very morning. They'd stayed in his head all day as he ran errands for Daniel Morris, toting important papers around town.

Wait. For how long? When would he know the right path?

He was on his way back to Daniel's office, several packets of papers in hand. Walking in the fresh air was good for his health, and while the work wasn't terribly challenging, he could never thank the man enough for giving him a chance. Walt had been in on it too, giving Tom a recommendation he wasn't sure he deserved.

He opened the door, pausing to give his eyes a moment to adjust.

After he'd blinked the interior of Daniel's office into focus and nodded to his boss behind the desk, he turned. And saw a familiar head of blond hair standing in front of one of Daniel's wall-to-wall bookcases.

Ida.

He froze in place. His suddenly nerveless fingers dropped the papers on Daniel's desk. He shifted to face her completely, barely breathing.

She had to be a dream. Or a mirage. He was so thirsty for the sight of her, it was as if he were dying in the desert and she a spring of cool water. An answered prayer.

She wore a pale blue dress and a short fawn-colored coat that accentuated the curve of her waist. Her cheeks were pink, and she was smiling at him. A tremulous smile.

"You're wearing my scarf," she said.

The door opened and closed behind him, and he knew Daniel had vacated the office to give them some privacy.

He had the scarf around his neck, though it hung down over both shoulders because it was warm today.

"I am." Was that his voice? Rough with emotion. He cleared his throat, but it didn't help. Everything he felt, everything he wanted to say, was lodged right there in a tight knot.

"Walt told me where to find you."

He was more than grateful to the man who had surprisingly become a friend.

"Why didn't you tell me?" she whispered.

He'd thought about it so many times. Written countless letters before crumpling them and tossing them in the fire.

Why had he been so foolish as to wait?

"I wanted to," he said. "I just wasn't sure..." He took a breath. "I didn't think I could do it at first. Make a new start." It was both easier and harder than he had expected, living on the right side of the law.

"And then I started to think that maybe I had just been a passing fancy to you. We didn't know each other very long—"

"Long enough. You're still wearing my scarf." She pulled something from her pocket. A small piece of cardboard with strings. "And I still have your thaumatrope. I think we've both spent long enough missing each other, don't you?"

He couldn't bear it any longer. He strode forward to reach for her. She came easily into his arms, her face already tilted up for his kiss.

This should've been their first kiss, the tentative, searching brush of his lips against hers. Though he couldn't regret anything that had passed between them in Bear Creek.

Her answering kiss was certain. She tasted of the future, and he wanted it.

She broke away first, beaming up at him. "Daniel will only be gone for a few minutes. He already warned me."

Tom didn't care. Ida's family, even the distant ones, were protective. As they should be. She was a treasure.

"I could hold you like this forever and be happy," he said. "I love you."

"I love you too."

His chest was so tight with happiness that he couldn't breathe.

She grinned up at him.

With his brothers behind bars and with the money Tom had saved living in a tiny flat and socking away every spare penny, forever stretched out ahead of him for the first time. With Ida by his side.

Her eyes were bright and still shone with emotion. "Do you think you could find fulfilling work in Bear Creek?"

The fact that she would ask made that suspicious lump in his throat return just as quickly as it had gone. He brushed her cheek with his thumb. "I thought you wanted to wait a while to settle down. Travel and do your nursing."

He would give her the world if he could. He had no intention of making her give up her dream.

"My sister-in-law Hattie wants to cut back her hours at the clinic. The workload is too much for Maxwell alone. He's asked me to work with him. I would probably need to live in town, but we could see the family as often as we wanted."

He'd formed a friendship with Walt. When he'd been under the Whites' roof, he had begun to think of Seb as a friend. Her other brothers might have to warm up to the idea of him in Ida's life. But if that was what she wanted...

"I'd be honored to go back home with you." His voice was choked as he forced out the next words. "I'd be doubly honored if you would agree to be my wife."

"Nothing would make me happier."

He kissed her again, even though he knew that Daniel would return any minute. He couldn't help himself. He loved her so much. And now he would have the chance to prove it every single day for the rest of his life.

This was the answer he'd been waiting for. The right path. At Ida's side.

―――――

NEW IN 2023...

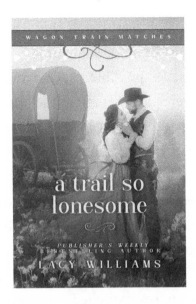

"What do you mean, she's gone?" Evangeline whispered the words, standing outside the wagon with her father. "How could Mrs. Fletcher just abandon us?"

Sara was still asleep in the tiny pallet Evangeline had created inside the wagon, atop all their supplies. Sara had outgrown her crib months ago in their stately townhouse back in Boston. But this was different. Aware of how high the wagon bed was from the ground, Evangeline had put Sara's pallet in between two trunks, with a barrel of salt pork and a smaller one of sugar barricading the girl in.

How could Sara sleep through all this ruckus? The thin line of silver at the horizon was the only sign that the sun was rising, but the camp was bustling and had been for some time.

It didn't seem possible that so many of their neighbors were awake after the raucous celebrating that had gone on long into the night. But the teenaged boy two wagons away was working to get his oxen into their braces one-by-one. The family just beyond him were eating breakfast. If Evangeline remembered correctly, their name was Fairfax. An older brother barely twenty, a sister in the middle, and a teen brother. And their aunt. Evangeline's nose twitched at the scent of fried ham.

Her father was loading the last of the crates into the rear of the wagon and she realized their time was short, but she couldn't wrap her mind around what he'd just informed her. Their cook, a long-time employee and one of the only women in Evangeline's life after her mother had passed, would not accompany them to Oregon.

"She didn't want to go in the first place," Father said without looking up.

"I know that," Evangeline returned. "But she promised. You *paid* her." Her father had offered the cook an exorbitant amount to come West with them. For good reason. Evangeline had never learned to cook. Father and Mother had always employed a cook. And a housekeeper, a groom for their horses, two maids.

Evangeline had spent almost a year preparing for this trip. Reading about what to expect on the trail. Making lists and buying what they needed. Taking riding lessons. Sewing lessons.

But she hadn't spent any time in the kitchen because Mrs. Fletcher was coming with them.

"It's not too late to rethink this plan of yours."

She kept her smile in place, though Father's words stung. Actually, it was too late to change her mind. Almost four years too late.

We have to go. She didn't give voice to the words. *Sara needs Oregon.* There was no future for Sara back in Boston. No future for Evangeline, either, but she'd resigned herself to that a long time ago. She could change things for Sara.

Evangeline knew how to win her father. "Just think of all the timber in Oregon," she said. "Every family on this wagon train will want lumber to buy to make a new house. And you'll provide it for them. Along with the families that come next year, and the year after."

Her father was a shrewd businessman, and they both knew she was right. Her father had built a series of successful mills under the tutelage of his father. The number of families traveling to Oregon with them was just the beginning. If there was a fortune to be made in Oregon, her father would be the one to make it.

He had listened to her opining about Oregon and the adventures—and the money—awaiting them on the other side of the country at the dinner table for nearly a week before she had won him over to the idea. She had been desperate, and he had finally seen the possibility.

He only glanced briefly at Evangeline. She ignored the pinch of hurt. "What will we eat for five months on the trail?"

"I'll cook."

It was still too dark to read her father's expression, but she could well imagine the skepticism she would see if there was light. Father didn't understand why this trip meant so much to her. "I'm certain I packed a cookbook."

He grunted. "Probably more than one," he muttered. "I'll start hitching up the oxen."

Evangeline had once been a spoiled girl, only worrying about the next fancy dress she would purchase for the next party. But that Evangeline had expired a long time ago. She straightened her shoulders and buoyed her resolve. How difficult could it be to cook over an open fire?

She took one last look at the skyline of Independence, now coming into relief as the first silver rays appeared on the horizon. She wouldn't let herself be frightened of this. There was no place for fear. Only courage.

"I don't suppose you've got an extra cord of rope." The oldest Fairfax brother was speaking to the neighbor between his wagon and Evangeline's.

She'd seen folks of all shapes and sizes in the meeting the other night. Stephen Fairfax seemed shy, had kept his head down during the brief introductions she and Father had made last night at camp.

She saw the slump of his shoulders and called out, "I have some extra rope."

She had packed the wagon meticulously, planned for a scenario just like this one. She and Father were perhaps at a disadvantage being from the city. But if she could help their neighbors and perhaps garner goodwill, surely it would make their journey easier at a later date.

She carefully stepped up into the wagon box, doing her best not to jostle the conveyance. She glanced to where Sara slept, though it was too dark inside the wagon to see anything other than a shadowy lump where she lay. Evangeline would have to wake the girl in a few minutes. They couldn't afford to stop for her to wash up as the wagons rolled out.

Evangeline reached into the small box that held the odds and ends she had packed as extras. She got back down from the wagon, waving the tied up rope like a prize.

"Thank you." His voice was fervent, though softer than she expected. She got her first good look at his face and realized he was younger than she'd thought. Much younger.

The smooth face with no hint of whiskers might belong to a 15-year-old. Surely she was mistaken. Maybe he was older but cursed by the fair skin he seemed to share with his sister. Some men didn't grow whiskers until an older age, right? Maybe he was even as old as seventeen. Not eighteen, surely?

He ducked his head and she realized she was staring. She cleared her throat. "You're welcome. I'm happy to help a neighbor."

He was gone before she could say anything else. She moved around to the back of the wagon, where the item she needed right now was packed away. She had to unlatch the tailgate and drag a box of ammunition out of the way before she found the crate she was looking for. It was packed with books, and she let her hand run over the spines of those at the top. She had packed and re-packed three crates just like this, her own personal library. She had filled every inch of space in each crate, re-arranging the books until not even a sheet of paper would fit between. She just knew there was a cookbook here.

"Pulling out in half an hour."

She nodded idly at the voice relaying the message, not looking up from what she was doing. Where was it?

"We won't wait if you're not ready. Half an hour." This time the starch in the male voice made her raise her head and look at him.

Leo Mason, the man who had been elected to captain for this first month of the journey. He had seemed resigned the other night; this morning he wore a stormy expression.

She abandoned her search for the cookbook and wiped her hand on her skirt before sticking it out and taking a few steps toward him. "I am Evangeline Murphy. My sister Sara is still sleeping, and my father is going to get the oxen. We'll be ready."

He stared at her hand doubtfully before he gave a limp handshake. "You have any problems, you can come to me."

"Or Owen. I remember."

His jaw tightened at the mention of his half brother. She had spent far too long last night remembering the tension between the two men during the meeting. Owen had seemed to take an ornery delight in announcing to the room that Leo was his half brother, as if anyone with eyes couldn't have seen the resemblance between them. She was an only child. When she had been young, she had often longed for a brother or sister. A companion to play with. Perhaps that was why she had spent so much time wondering at the broken relationship in a family of strangers.

"You'll want to keep the little one up in the wagon till we get clear of the creek." He pointed to a line of trees in the distance.

She didn't see a creek, but maybe he knew the landscape she didn't.

He started to walk off—without giving her a chance to say anything else—but seemed to change his mind. "It's not too late for you to decide to stay."

She bristled. "What does that mean?"

"You don't look like you belong here."

How dare he? Her temper sparked hot prickles all up and down her arms. "I belong here as much as you or anyone else," she blurted.

He walked off, shaking his head.

And she was left trembling with anger.

The nerve of the man. He might not think Evangeline looked like a pioneer, but she had determination. If she had learned anything from her father in years of watching him do business, determination was all she needed.

———

LEO KNOCKED his hat back on his head.

He should've let Owen win the vote for captain. It'd been a snap decision, but his stubborn pride hadn't wanted Owen in a position of authority over him. A stance he now regretted.

They hadn't even pulled out and he'd been called on to settle a dispute between two families. A dog had gotten loose of the rope it'd been tied to and eaten the neighbors' breakfast.

And he'd clearly offended Evangeline Murphy by his suggestion that she wasn't fit for this trip. Maybe it wasn't his business, but he didn't want to spend months alongside someone whose ignorance would cost them time and extra work. Those shoes! They were fit for a ballroom maybe, but he could almost guarantee she'd have blisters up and down her feet by lunchtime.

He wondered, not for the first time, if they'd made the right decision leaving New Jersey. It'd seemed the only decision in the face of the trouble Coop had stirred up. But this journey was a massive undertaking. He wouldn't have a moment's rest, not when he'd be watching over Alice and making sure Coop stayed in line.

Alice had barely stirred when he'd left the tent over an hour ago. Coop had been hungover and hadn't said a word to Leo, while Collin, always the peacemaker, had quietly gone about breaking camp. Why couldn't Coop be more like his twin?

The farther West they traveled, the better. There would be no saloons once they hit the plains. Leo had been careful to ensure no casks made it on board; not even for medicinal purposes.

He made his way through the wagons, the level of noise rising each moment. The folks traveling were excited; they hadn't had a taste of hardship yet. It'd be a quieter start tomorrow, he guessed.

A shrill whistle caught his attention. Hollis waved him over to a wagon outfitted and ready to go, the oxen in their traces. A man in fancy duds, dark pants and vest with a crisp white shirt that stood out in the breaking dawn, was with Hollis. Who was that?

Leo drew up short when he got within spitting distance. He knew that city slicker.

"I'm adding one more wagon to your company," Hollis said in lieu of a greeting. "Mr. Braddock joined up yesterday. I checked over his gear and everything seems to be in order."

Leo's eyes narrowed at the slightly younger man. He didn't move closer or attempt to shake the man's hand. What was this? A ploy? No hint of any lawmen Robert Braddock brought with him. Leo had believed they were free and clear of Braddock and his grandfather and the life they'd left behind in New Jersey.

Apparently not.

Hollis looked between the two men when silence reigned for too long. "Problem?"

Braddock stared at Leo. He could probably get Leo's family kicked off the wagon train with a few words about Coop. But he only stared, his expression hard.

And Leo didn't want Hollis to know about Coop's trouble.

"You know how to drive those oxen?" Leo asked, forcing his tone into something polite.

The other man's jaw worked. "I'll make do."

"We're rolling out soon." Hollis strode away and left the two of them standing there, still staring.

"What do you want?" Maybe Leo shouldn't have growled the words, but seeing Braddock again had his heart pounding and his senses on high alert. Braddock had been the one to call for the police that terrible night at the powder mill. He'd been a part of the event that had set this whole thing in motion, sent Leo and his family far away from the only home they'd known.

"I'd like to speak to Alice," Braddock's words were guarded, his expression stoic.

No. The instant denial sprang to Leo's lips, but he stifled it as a memory of Alice, her face stained with soot and tears, held their friend Ellen in a crying heap. Ellen's husband had died in the explosion that night.

Braddock wasn't getting close to Alice or any of Leo's family.

"Whatever you've got to say, you can say it to me."

There was a crack in Braddock's calm expression. "I'll speak to Alice first."

The man's stubbornness only intensified Leo's resolve not to let him anywhere near his sister.

"If you came all this way for a chat, I'll have to ask you to move your wagon. We're getting ready to move."

Braddock's eyes sparked. "I aim to get to Oregon, same as you. Where's Alice?"

In the bustle of the morning, Leo hadn't noticed someone sidling up to him, but now a tall figure stepped beside him, facing Braddock.

Owen crossed his arms over his chest, looking menacing. "What's going on?"

Braddock's gaze moved between them. "Who're you?" he demanded.

"Who're you?" Owen returned. "If you're a part of this wagon train, you'd better mount up."

In the distance, a bugle sounded. A dog bayed, and from an even further distance, a weapon discharged.

Braddock eyed the two of them. Just when Leo thought he would keep arguing, he turned to boost himself into the seat of his wagon

Leo skirted Braddock's wagon. If they were pulling out, he wanted to be on horseback.

Unfortunately, Owen followed. Several wagons were rolling slowly forward, and Leo made sure to move quickly out of their way.

"I didn't need your help," he muttered. Owen already knew too much about what had transpired in New Jersey. He and August had walked into their lives at just the wrong time.

"Thanks for your help, brother," Owen mimed, as if Leo had said the words.

Leo's temper sparked. "We're not brothers," he burst out. He turned to face Owen squarely and his hand fisted at his side.

It was like looking at his father all over again, though his memories of the man were hazy. Maybe not memories at all.

"You don't want me in your life, but too bad. August and I *are* your family."

Leo shook his head.

"You're gonna need us before this journey is over." Owen made the words sound like a threat, one that Leo immediately wanted to refute.

Until he realized someone was shadowing them. His face flushed with heat as he turned to acknowledge the slight figure behind them.

Evangeline, and she looked as if she wished she was anywhere else.

"We'll finish this later," Owen muttered before he stalked off.

No, they wouldn't.

He worked to clear the traces of anger from his expression. "You need something?" Maybe he hadn't been able to eradicate every trace of frustration because she balked at his impatient tone.

She had something clutched to her chest and now brought it out to show it to him. It looked like some kind of journal. Even if he'd been able to read, he wouldn't have been able to make out the scrawled handwriting she showed him.

"I wanted to ask whether we'll be staying the night at Cow Hollow creek, or if we'll go five miles farther, to the meadow described in this guidebook."

That's what she wanted to know? Right now, while they were pulling out?

"We'll pass the night where Hollis tells us."

"I was just wondering, because the guidebooks say—"

He cut her off with a sharp wave of his hand through the air between them. "Ma'am, you'd do best right now to worry about your little sister. Make sure she's safe in the wagon. There's a lot of animals moving around, and if she were to get stepped on, it'd be bad."

Color rose in her cheeks. Her lips pinched, and he was sorry if he'd hurt her feelings, but he didn't have time for this right now.

READ A TRAIL SO LONESOME

ALSO BY LACY WILLIAMS

Wagon Train Matches series

A Trail So Lonesome

Trail of Secrets

A Trail Untamed

Wind River Hearts series

Marrying Miss Marshal

Counterfeit Cowboy

Cowboy Pride

The Homesteader's Sweetheart

Courted by a Cowboy

Roping the Wrangler

Return of the Cowboy Doctor

The Wrangler's Inconvenient Wife

A Cowboy for Christmas

Her Convenient Cowboy

Her Cowboy Deputy

Catching the Cowgirl

The Cowboy's Honor

Winning the Schoolmarm

The Wrangler's Ready-Made Family

Christmas Homecoming

Heart of Gold

Sutter's Hollow series (contemporary romance)

His Small-Town Girl

Secondhand Cowboy

The Cowgirl Next Door

Hometown Sweethearts series (contemporary romance)

Kissed by a Cowboy

Love Letters from Cowboy

Mistletoe Cowboy

The Bull Rider

The Brother

The Prodigal

Cowgirl for Keeps

Jingle Bell Cowgirl

Heart of a Cowgirl

3 Days with a Cowboy

Prodigal Cowgirl

Soldier Under the Mistletoe

The Nanny's Christmas Wish

The Rancher's Unexpected Gift

Someone Old

Someone New

Someone Borrowed

Someone Blue (newsletter subscribers only)

Ten Dates

Next Door Santa

Always a Bridesmaid

Love Lessons

Cowboy Fairytales series (contemporary fairytale romance)

Once Upon a Cowboy

Cowboy Charming

The Toad Prince

The Beastly Princess

The Lost Princess

Kissing Kelsey

Courting Carrie

Stealing Sarah

Keeping Kayla

Melting Megan

The Other Princess

The Prince's Matchmaker

Not in a Series

Wagon Train Sweetheart (historical romance)

ACKNOWLEDGMENTS

With thanks to Shelley Crews and Lillian Bristol for proofreading.

And a special thank you to the over 1,000 readers who submitted names for the children of my characters that needed naming. The names I selected were suggested by:

Ruth F.
Patrician Ann N.
June J.
Helen P.
Melanie C.
Tabitha V.
Anita R.
Mary Katherine S.
Julie Y.
Sandi B.

Thank you for every single suggestion. I've kept the list for future books!

A SPECIAL THANK YOU FOR
MY READERS

There never seem to be enough words to say thank you for being one of my fabulous readers. After more than a decade of publishing, it's high time I recognize some of my most devoted fans. I would like to personally thank the following readers (list in alphabetical order by first name):

Abby Zimmel, Alesha Oliver Lane, Amy Barr, Amy Marie, Amy S., Amy Smith, Angela Reynolds, Angeline Farrow-Douglas, Anita Jamros, Anita R, Anita Reeves Kirk, Anita Vogt, Ann Carvan, Ann F., Ann Stromsness, Ann Williams, Ann-Frances Mahar Herndon, Anne Powell, Annette kelly, Annika Terese, Ashlyn Z, Autumne Burks, Barb Austinson, Barb King, Barbara B, Barbara Robinson, Barbara S Thorn, Barbara V., Barbara Watts, Barbara Balaban, Becki Smith, Beth Fullerton, Beth Helm, Beth Heydn, Beth Riggen, BETH Z, Betty Alderfer, Betty Finch, Betty Spradlin, Bev D, Beverly, Bil Fuller, Bill Barry, Bobbie T, Bonnie, Bonnie Steinhoff, Brandi Moffett, Brenda Dickson,

Bridgette S, Bud Bivens, Bunny Albright, bunny-doodles, C Dove, C. Wicker, Caren J Silverberg, Carl B - Skip, Carlene, CARLENE MILLER, Carol D-D, Carol McConnaughey Boyle, Carolyn Bryant, Carolyn Lester, Carolyn P., Carolyn Payne, Carrie Taylor, Catarina K, Cathy B, Cathy Larson, Cecelia's "Cece", Chandalyn, Charee Levering, Charee Viola Levering, Charlene Zall Capodice, Cheryl Lee, Cheryl Mickelson, Chris Meiser, Christina Smith, Christina Woody, Cindy Joy, Cindy Poole Hope, Cindy Stimmel, Claire Smith, Clara Page, Colleen Laginess, Colleen Lynch, Colleen T, Cyndi C, Cynthia Whitman, D. J. Rothe, Danyelle Wadsworth, Dar, Darla Stapleton, Darlene Custer, David Carswell, Dawn Roth Resar, Deanna Newman, Debbie A., Debbie B, Debbie Griffin, Debbie Hammer, Debbie Hughes, Debbie W, Debbie Waring, Deborah Gould, Deborah Hazelton, Deborah L. Dumm, Debra Eberhart, Debra Lynn Parker, Debra Morgan, Debra Phelps, Debra Pruss, Debra Rylander, Debra Schinkel, Dellas, Denise L, Denise Martin, Denman Barry, Diane Wasko, Diane Wilson, Dianna Lloyd, DJ Porter, Donna H, Donna Hall Griffin, Doris J. Bernethy, Edwina Kiernan, EJ Derenzy, Elizabeth Jackson, Elizabeth van Rensburg, Elouise Lord, Emily Gilmer, Esther K, Fabi Duran, Fellicia Ortiz, Fran Scruggs, Gael, Gail Ann

Williams, Gail Hollingsworth, Gale Canzoneri, Gennifer A Winger, Georgia Johnson, Ginger G, Glenna West, Heather Sexton, HeidiLorin Callies, helen mudd, Holly Vee, Irina A, JackieT, Jamie H, Jan Smith, Jan Swanson, Jane Marler, Jane Moeggenberg, JaneFW, Janet Demaree, Janet Everett, Janet Jolley, Janet L, Janet La Grasta, Janet Sanchez, Janette Scanlan, Jasmine M., Jeanne DeLoca Poland, Jenn C., Jenn Kolacinski Neitzke, Jennie Lee Ersari, Jennifer Cleaveland, Jennifer Tremeer, Jenny-Lynn Fricke, Jerry P., Jessie L. Bell, Jewel Young, Jill A. Vatter, Jo-Ann Toth, Joan L., Joan M Lebo, Jodie Sue Davis, John K., Johnnie M., Joy Clark, Joyce Belle Pauley-Clifton, Judith A. Fritz, Judy B. Fordham, Judy Golden, Judy Gottschalk, Judy K Inscho, Judy Powell, Julie Faulkenberry, Julie J, Julie Tiedemann, Julieanne Canny, Kaitlyn Reusser, Kalena, Kara Nettles, Karen Miracle, Karen Semones, Karen Steele, Karyn Rassel, Karyn S., Kat Taylor, Kathleen Merryman, Kathryn M Smith, Kathryn McQueeny, Kathy Adamski, Kathy Anderson, Kathy Blood, Kathy Dunn, Kay, Kay B, Kay R., Kerry Bell, Kim Brougher, Kimberly Klauburg, Kimberly W., Kitty Elder, Kris B, Kunita Gear, LaFonia Michael, LaRae Galloway, Laura Dudek, Laura Hart, Laura West, Laurie Kirk, Lawrence Grogan, Lenora Littlejohn,

Lerryn, Letha Armstrong, Linda Carey, Linda Christmas, Linda F, Linda Farabaugh, Linda G, Linda L Bush, Linda M, Linda May, Linda McFarland, LINDA MERSC, Linda S. Ward, Linda Stahr, Lisa Egnew, Lisa Poisson, Lisa Venter, Lora Musikantow, Lori Cole, Lori Ferry, Lori R, Lorraine Patterson, Louise Bateman, Lucia Poorman, Lydia Erickson, Lynda O., Lynette Fegley, Lynn Tolles, Lynne Myers, Maggie Sunflower Vargas, Maratha Barton, Margaret Diane Johnson, Margarete S. -M., Margie Evans Taylor, Margie Harris, Maria Blodgett, Marilú Wright, Marilyn D Carrion, Marilyn Rushing, Marlee LeAnne, Mary or Mary Kathryn, Mary Ann S., Mary Ann Speel, Mary Ann V., Mary Gerrish, Mary K Anderson, Mary Kopitar, Mary Martin, Mary Samida, MarylanS, Mel Mel, Melanie M., Melissa Hartwell, Melody Rekow, Melody Tregear, Michele B, Michele Miracle, Michelle Dodge, Michelle Fidler, Mindy E., Misty G, Myaisha J., Mykaliah, Myra Few, Myrna Araujo-Constantine, Nancy C, Nancy J, Nancy S-W, Nancy Tackett, Nancy Volk, natalie rae, Natasha wall, Naya Wood, Nikki Nance, Nikki Stewart, Nikkie Wallerstein, Nioma Jane Strength, Paige Newsom, Pam Chandler, Pamela S., Patrice S, Patricia D, Patricia Grupe Guyette, Patsy S., Patti Arteaga, Paul E. Harris, Paula Holderfield, Paulette Amonson, Pauline Frost,

Peggy B, Penny A., Penny L, Pete Johanson, Phyllis B, Prinsesa Elsa, Priscila P., Rachel Branigan, Raven Randall, Renee Blamer, Renee D., Renee McDonald, Renita Kelly, Rhonda Cooper, Roani Bester, Rob Albury, RobbyeFaye, Robyn Lee Snyder, Rosanne, Rose M Johnson, Rosemarie A., Rosemarie M., Ruth E, Ruth Fiser, Sally Childs, Sally P, Sally W, Sandi Ben, Sandra McCandless, Sandra Watson, Sarabeth Jenkins, Sarah DeLong, Sarah Hume, SARAH TAYLOR, Shan Jones, Sharon Chilton Traulsen, Sharon Meier, Sheila Bryant, Sheila S., Sheila Stern, Shelia Williams, Shelley M, Sherri Tutor, Sherry A. Toelle, Sherry Meyd, Sheryl Barlage, Shirley Holt, Shushu, Sonia Nesbeth, Sonja Nishimoto, Stacey Handzus, Stella Valdez, Stephanie M. Watson, Stephanie Halcomb, Stephanie O., Stephanie S., Sue Ellen Woodham, Susan Impastato, Susan Nuss, Susan Pacheco, Sydney W, Sylvia Gwen, Sylvia Gwen, Tammy Conatser, Tanya arehart, Tanya Kurtin, Teena White-Miller, Teresa M, Teresa Mauder, Terri Ayers, Tiffany Clouse, Tina M Sorensen, Tina Rinehart, Tony Yannuzzi, Tracey Lewis, Tracie Joyner, Tracy Watson, Trila Butler, Trish O., Valri Western, Vicki Hodges, Vickie B., Vickie L, Vicky L. McQuiston, Virginia Campbell, Vivian Gelber, Wendy A., William Fuller, Yvonne M.

CPSIA information can be obtained
at www.ICGtesting.com
Printed in the USA
BVHW080358240323
661050BV00002B/116